Camou flage

SELASSIE MENSAH

Camou flage

SELASSIE MENSAH

Camouflage

This Novel is a work of fiction. Names, characters, places and
incidents are either the product of the author's imagination or
are used fictitiously. Any resemblance to actual events, locales,
organisations, or persons, living or dead, is entirely
coincidental and beyond the intent of either the author or
publisher.

ISBN: 978-9988-8752-8-2

Designed and Printed in Ghana
by Sedesel

Published by Sedesel
PMB 40, Madina, Accra
+233 26 350 7779, 050 136 8890
Email: sedeselpublications@gmail.com

To

Auntie Aba (Mrs. Aba Brew-Hammond), my lecturer.
Thank you for the love, support and encouragement.

CHAPTER ONE

Chopbox Blessings

"Eiiii Sompa, come and see o, come and see what the Lord has done!" Naomi screamed for her friend to come to the balcony. The whole hall seemed to be in an uproar at whatever Naomi was excited about.

"What is it?" Sompa run to her side. She wondered if Naomi had seen an angel in broad daylight.

"See…see that boy with the chopbox. Aden? Does he still think he's in SHS? Anaa his parents forgot? I won't be surprised if we find lots and lots of gari and shito in that chopbox. Bringing a chopbox here, I don't think they would forget that," she said laughing as she pointed out the new arrival to her.

The boy that Sompa saw did not look like a boy at all. He was all man and she was sure that under different circumstances, the ladies in the hall would have been drooling over him and the guys will either be jealous or try to befriend him. He certainly looked like one of the guys in the viral *Kupe* video on Instagram that every girl seemed to crush on.

The taxi driver helped the guy take his chopbox out of the boot. The guy's shoulders sagged and he looked crestfallen at the amount of attention he was receiving. He glanced accusingly at his mother who was dressed in kaba and slit. She seemed very content to see her son safely in school and proud that he had gained admission to the University. She was very oblivious of the attention.

As they made their way to his room on the part of the hall for the guys, there were jeers and catcalls and people didn't miss the chance to capture the University guy carrying his SHS guy self to his room. Naomi didn't leave herself out as she eagerly took several pictures of the chopbox.

She snickered and glanced at Sompa who looked amused and unconcerned at the same time.

"This would make the campus news!" Naomi said excitedly. She couldn't wait to read what would be written about him. She was sure they'd even interview him.

Sompa would have laughed if she was in another year but right now, all she felt was pity for the guy. She was reminded of how clueless she had been when she first stepped on campus and entered the Sankofa Hall.

The Sankofa Hall was painted just like the petals of the Edelweiss flower. It was clean and white through and through. However, ironically, the flowers that adorned the compound of the hall were chrysanthemums and hibiscuses. It was known as the quietest hall on campus. Sompa was yet to experience that quiet because lately she had been receiving uninvited guests into her room.

The buildings of the University were so big and the environment so huge it felt like they were in another world. She felt really small in a big sea with big fishes. She still couldn't believe she had made it to the University considering all the challenges she and her parents had to overcome and the money they had to get to secure admission for her. She was really grateful to God for his faithfulness because she knew that without Him she wouldn't have been there by now.

She had made many promises to God, all of them were recorded in her diary. She had made a list of things she wanted to do right in her life for she didn't want any regrets.

1. Stay faithful to God
2. Make great friends
3. Be a good student and get a first class
4. No boyfriends and I mean none.

There were more but she also knew that laughing at the guy with the chopbox wasn't a great way to start.

"Eii, there are people and there are 'people'," Naomi said, stretching on the last 'people' as she followed Sompa back into the room. "See it's all over social media: Boy brings Chopbox to University."

"Derrr norr," Sompa commented and smiled

as she settled back on her bed. Naomi wasn't her roommate but her classmate from St. Theresa Girls Senior High School. Even then they were not friends – Sompa didn't even remember ever uttering 'hi' to her back then. However, when Naomi and Sompa met on their first day in the hall, they hit it off like disparate allies with a common enemy.

Sompa also felt comfortable with Naomi because she seemed to know her way around campus since she'd visited her big brother lots of times in the University. Her brother, Nolan was in final year now, pursuing Architecture and Sompa had already met him. Nolan was a very funny guy and had made her feel at home instantly. Part of her wished they had come to University earlier because now, Nolan was preparing to finish with school.

Sompa's room served three people and she wondered when her other roommate was going to come. One roommate had already arrived when she came in but after introducing herself as Reinee, who was from Gabon, the girl had given her a cold shoulder. She hoped and prayed that the others weren't like that else she was going to have to stay with Naomi.

After replying some messages on her phone, she turned back to the Korean series she was watching whiles Naomi smiled at her phone, obviously giggling at a message she had read. *Boys over Flowers* was the hot Kdrama on now. She had fallen in love a thousand times with Gu Jun Pyo and she had often wished she was in Nam Di's shoes.

Naomi hated Kdramas because they always had this obvious storyline- the characters start out as enemies, they become friends, and they fall in love but hide behind their feelings until the end when they get married. The 'no kissing' in Kdramas wasn't real and that made the whole movie too fantastical.

"Kissing is part of life and when there's love and no kissing it isn't real for me," Naomi always defended. She preferred telenovelas where she would see real action.

Sompa was getting into an interesting part of

the series when she heard a knock on her door. The knock was hard and incessant.

"Who is that carpenter knocking on the door like that?" Naomi raised her voice as she scowled at the door. She loved to make friends but this was pushing it too far. Since Sompa came, her door had had no peace. She felt if the door were to be a human being it would be terribly injured and would be crying out in pain.

Sompa pressed her finger to her lips at Naomi and grunted as she got up to answer the door. At the door stood a young man and a lady who wore friendly smiles and wielded Bibles. She was sure about what they were going to say but let them in anyway.

"Hi, Hello," they greeted as they came in. She offered them seats and Naomi gave them the once over that seemed to say, 'We've heard what you are coming to say already so I'm not going to listen.'

"My name is Rhoda and I'm Isaac, we're here to share the Word of God with you. Let us share a word of prayer."

After their prayer, Rhoda shared her

experiences with them.

"Two years ago, I was just like you. So naïve about life on campus and I'll say that it hasn't been easy. Living on campus and living in SHS is a different ball game all together. In SHS, you have the bell to wake you up and housemistresses to discipline you but over here you discipline yourself. Remember that you aren't just here on admission, you are also here on a mission. Take your studies seriously but don't think that is the only reason you came here. A certain guy graduated here with First Class to his honour and got the highest GPA ever to be recorded in Ghanaian Tertiary Education. He was hugely honoured and recognized at the graduation ceremony but ask me, if he had any friends to celebrate with him. He spent all of his years on campus holed up in the library or the study room and didn't make any impact on people," she continued, "God wants you to live a balanced and fulfilled life. Choose your friends wisely and get to know God's will and purpose in your life. And don't attend every activity or event on campus, be picky and use your time wisely. You and I know that time waits for no man, therefore use your time profitably. And one more thing don't compare yourselves with others. Stay true to who you are and whose you are and make sure to learn hard. You don't want to be disappointing God when you get a Second Class Upper/Lower knowing that you can be a first class student bringing honour and glory to God."

Sompa listened intently to their advice and hoped that her stay at the University would be fruitful. After they prayed and left them, she knew she couldn't spoil the new lease of life and zeal with neither the Korean people nor the Spanish people.

———————————————

Mama always does this? Why? Why? Elikem thought when he was finally in his room away from the prying eyes who wanted to get a last look at his chopbox, which had probably made him the most popular first year student in the University or possibly in the whole history of University life and tertiary education.

He hated the amount of attention he was getting. How was he supposed to concentrate when he and his mum had virtually announced to the whole world that he was not cool? His roomies were even amused when they saw the chopbox. One of them had helped him to carry the thing into the room amidst fits of giggles. He laughed so hard that he was barely able to help in the holding.

"I hope say shito den gari dey chaw," one tall, scrawny looking guy said, covering his mouth to control the giggles, "Abi Caleb but my friends all dey bell me Broomstick. I'm in third year doing Mechanical Engineering. The guy who just helped you is Steven, Fawohodie Park is his second home and pulpit, and he's the SU President in this room, after some time you'll come to know why. He's in third year pursuing Akan. Joey is the one who is out. He's in final year doing Chemical Engineering. What course are you doing?"

"Pharmacy," he said in the most confident tone that he could muster.

"That's nice, you can even start doing commer in pharmacy with your chopbox, I'm sure it will be a good start."

"Broomstick, *gyae gimmie no*," Steven scolded.

"Oh what, I just want to make him feel comfortable."

But comfortable wasn't close to what he was feeling right now. He had to hide away till this Chopbox wahala case died down. Being a celebrity all because of a chopbox wasn't cool.

His phone rang very loudly, the kind of phone that cried to let everyone know that this was a yam from China. It was his mum.

"Hello Mama."

"Hello my son, have you settled?"

"Yes, I have."

"Have you started making friends?"

"Mummy, I only just arrived and thanks to the chopbox you made me bring to a University, I don't think I will be making any friends now."

"Oh stop talking like that. Remember to eat well. Always cook and learn very hard; I don't want your errant father to think that I didn't do a good job. Please learn hard and make me proud."

"Ok Mama, bye."

"Oh and let me know the books you need, I love you, my boy."

"I luh-" he began to say but stopped when he looked up and saw Broomstick smirking at him.

CHAPTER TWO

Broken Chains

Araba stuck her head out of the four-wheeler as it drove through the university. She breathed in the fresh rushing air of freedom which was slightly spiced with the scent of the tropical trees that adorned the streets of the school.

She just couldn't wait to see her hall, meet her roommates and begin this journey altogether. She was mighty glad for school but not in the reason you hope. She chose this school because it was far from home, practically out in another region and far from the eyes of her parents. No more wondering about what they thought, she was going to enjoy and experience all the things this place had to offer and she meant all. It wasn't easy getting out of that house and most especially, out of that SHS prison. She hated the rules, the limitations, and most importantly, she wasn't going to miss the school menu which featured unexciting dishes like Gas and Kenkey, the okro stew which students mournfully called, 'Count your blessings' and the eggstew they called 'Baby Shit'. She wasn't going to miss the constant fights and 'wars' over small Sunday Jollof. She wasn't going to miss that place where they treated her like a person sentenced to four years of hard labour. This place just broke her chains.

"Woohooo!" she screamed in the air as the car made its way to the front of her hall. The choice of halls was also a decision she made. She had heard so much noise about the Central Hall, especially their hot, steamy, and crazy events, their hall week celebrations, pageants and jamming hall fairs. Stonebwoy's *Mane me* welcomed her into the hall as soon as she stepped out of the car with her luggage.

"Thank you," she said to the driver who helped her carry her stuff to the porter's lodge. Checking in was a long and tiring process that she wished for a moment that she had come along with her parents.

"I'll be fine," she assured herself as she let out a big sigh. She had to stand in a long queue for her passport pictures to be taken, fill in some forms and show and sign some documents before she was handed the keys to her room. She wondered how her roommates would be like. She hoped that they would be fun roomies. She didn't want boring, dull, bookish roomies or worse, the Bible freaks. Araba considered herself a Christian; her dad was even the founder and pastor of their local church in Ashie but Jesus freaks made her feel so unholy and uncomfortable in her own skin. She prayed that such roomies wouldn't be her portion; although she doubted God would answer such a prayer. He was too busy solving big problems like wars and famine, He wouldn't bother minding her.

"Hello," a voice called. Araba looked up and saw a young man staring down at her. His pearly white teeth and bright eyes nearly got her dazed. He was so tall that she had to look up at him. He had beautiful eyes and a dark skin and he looked like he went to the gym every day.

"Hi, you are in first year right?"

"Yeah," she answered, "It's that obvious huh?"

He laughed and nodded. His laughter was deep and warm. She liked the sound of it.

"C'mon let me help you with your stuff. Where are they?"

"I left them at the porter's lodge."

"Okay, then let's go and get them," he continued, "What's your room number?"

"Room 64, West Wing. Where in the world is that?"

He chuckled, "Follow me."

When they finally got to her room with her things, Araba thanked him and was about to close the door when he stopped her.

"Wait, I didn't quite catch your name."

She laughed, "That's because you never asked me and I never told you. You aren't asking now either."

"My bad." He scratched his head and gave her one of his winsome smiles again. "Ok, so what's your name?"

"Araba."

"Mhmmm Fante, that's nice. I'm Joey." He asked, "Can I have your number?"

"You are very brave oh, *anka menfa ma wo.* But since you helped and are asking nicely I will give it to you."

Then she rattled off the numbers to him as he calmly entered them on his phone. "Thanks, I'll give you a call." Joey smiled.

"Welcome," she returned his smile as she closed the door. She leaned on the door to revel in the moment before she went exploring. She didn't see Joey's jubilation behind the door.

Araba noticed that one of her roommates had already picked out a down bed which was away from the door. She took in the amount of shoes displayed under her roommate's bed and already formed a perception about her roommate.

"Wei dierrr, oyɛ high-class girl o. Hwɛ ne shoes." After oohing and aahing over them, she began to unpack her stuff and settle down. She was bone-tired from the journey. But before that she had to eat. She brought out the fried rice she had bought on the way and was about to put the fork to her lips when she heard a knock on her door. She was expecting to see her roommate but at the door, were a group of three; two ladies and one guy all wearing bright warm smiles. She wondered what they were doing there because she could already smell Jesus on them.

"Hello, good morning."

"Good morning."

"Hope you are fine?"

"Yes I am."

"We are here to share God's word with you. Can we come in?"

She was tired. Maybe she should just listen to whatever they had to say and send them on their way. She opened the door wide to let them in.

"Oh, I see that you have just arrived," one of them commented and she nodded, too tired to give them the pleasure of hearing her voice.

"You are welcome to University of Nsoroma," one girl said, "Anyway we are glad that you have arrived safely. We want to share the Word of God with you. I'm Sandra and these are my colleagues, Shally and Emmanuel. What's your name?"

"I'm Araba Hammond."

"Ooh nice! We want to ask you a question. Are you born again?"

"Yes I am, I accepted Jesus Christ into my life and all of that."

"Oh that's great. Then it looks like we are halfway done with what we came here for. We just want you to be cautious and tread softly in this university, and especially this hall. Don't forget the place you came from. Don't forget your identity."

"Okay," she said smiling but only she knew that she wasn't going to heed to all the advice they were doling out to her. She had already forgotten where she was from the moment she stepped on campus. She wasn't going to let these people spoil her mood.

"That's good, which church do you attend?"

"Christ Apostolic Church."

"Oh really? That's the same church we attend."

"Oh ok." She tried to be happy about that piece of information.

"We meet every Wednesdays for our midweek service and every Sundays for church service at the Central Hall on Thursdays and Sundays. On Thursdays, service starts at 6:30pm -9:00pm and Sundays, 6:30 am- 10:30am. This Sunday is going to be our first meeting in the semester."

"Okay." She stared at them blankly wielding herself not to say anything more. Like she would spend that much time in church!

"Can we have your number?" the guy asked, pulling out his phone.

She itched to give a 'No' but called them out on a second thought.

"Thank you so much, we will be coming around to check up on you from time to time," they said.

"Okay, thank you for passing by." She stood up with them and led them to the door. She let out a big sigh after closing the door on them.

She chuckled under her breath. Church! Perhaps once in a while. She just couldn't see herself wake up that early for church. She just hoped her phone wouldn't be ringing from calls from those Jesus freaks and with that disturbing thought, she went back to eating.

CHAPTER THREE

Love on the streets

Sompa gaped at the guy who stood before her as he stared intently into her eyes. He was a very fair guy with glasses on and a head that was shaped like the front of a bicycle; that's how it looked like in Sompa's mind. His glasses were designer blue Ray Bans and he had some matching sneakers on. He waited desperately for her response after he had introduced himself as Theodore, a final year student pursuing Mathematics, who was deeply in love with her. He had professed his love for her right across the street where she had been standing waiting for Naomi.

They were already late for the late afternoon programme at the Central Hall all thanks to

Naomi. The programme was organized to make students aware of the various clubs and societies on campus. She wished she hadn't given out her number now that she knew he was crazy.

Love at first sight only happened in telenovelas like *Mari Cruz*; not in real life. She was still in shock as the guy waited expectantly for her response.

"Uh…okay…" Sompa could barely get the words out of her mouth.

"Is that all you have to say to what I just said?"

"I guess, because I don't think we should move on that fast," she said, "I can only be your friend."

"Sure, of course we can start as friends and develop into something better; another level kraa." He continued, "Is it a crime to tell someone that you love them?"

"It is when you are strangers and you just met the person across the street. And for the record, who goes about loving people? You've got to know them first, what if I'm a serial killer or gold digger?"

"I really doubt that."

"Please you should. Innocent people are the most dangerous that is why Satan himself does not come around as the red scary demon with vampire ears, sharp teeth and a tail," she ranted on, feeling it was her duty to school him.

"Eheh?" Theodore said, still smiling as if she had just intrigued him the more.

"Yes," she said in a tone that warned him to back off.

She turned to see Naomi walking as slowly as she could as if the entire world was waiting for the queen. Naomi waved her over sheepishly, already sending silent apologies with her gaze.

"Ooh great, my friend has arrived. I'm late I have to go," she said and walked away hurriedly without waiting for a response.

"I'll call you," she heard the guy shout in the distance.

"Who was that?" Naomi asked as they walked to the Central Hall.

"Some guy bi who has fallen in love at the mere sight of me."

"And what did he want?"

"It's obvious he was thinking I'll say yes and marry him just across the street."

Naomi laughed, "Hahahaaaa, looks like he asked the wrong girl."

"Where were you, Nao?"

"I was dressing up. Tara, you know my unserious roomie who is doing medicine? She was doing my makeup and hair for me."

"Makeup? Just for this small meeting?"

"Herh, Sompa, a lady must be prepared at all times. It's very important oh. I don't know where I will meet my future husband so every day before I go out, I must look stunning."

"If he really is your husband, shouldn't he like you without it?" Sompa asked and Naomi shrugged, "Yoo, because of your efforts for your future husband, we are late. We better run before the rain pours."

"Heheheeeee, don't run too fast. If we are late just let's be late. That's my philosophy."

"And apparently it's this same philosophy that makes you late for class no matter how many hours late you set your time. Let's not pass the

Broad Way; the boys will shout nonsense at us."

"Why are you scared? Oh Sompa, you are scared…" Naomi teased.

"No I'm not scared, I'm just not in the mood to hear ridiculous things. Do you know that one girl in my class cried because she was taking that route and a boy shouted, *'lady ena wo nante te se dabodabo. Enfata wo kraa'*. And that all her *kaikai* face, where was she taking it to. Was she starting Halloween in Ghana? That Broad way dierrr the things you hear can be enough to break a woman's confidence."

"And that's where our favourite waakye and Gobɛ is too. I'm not scared of those boys. One day, I'll give them a clapback of their lives, they'll never forget," Naomi said determinedly.

_____

"Ooh la! La!" came the sharp, loud voice that woke Sompa up. She had just returned from the programme with Naomi and after a bowl of icecream, Naomi had returned to her room next door.

She had dozed off. She opened her eyes to see Reinee standing by her bed, so excited. Wow, she had never seen this girl smile before ever since she stepped into the room.

Heck, she didn't even know that Reinee had a laughter or humour bone in her.

"Hmm, what is it?"

"Come and see, come and see, I cannot say it in words."

Sompa grudgingly got off the top bunk bed and removed her cover cloth. She rubbed her eyes and yawned.

This better be something I will be excited about, she thought as she hurriedly wore her slippers.

Reinee was in her nightie and had her towel and sponge around her and she wore a shower cap. She looked like she had just stepped out of the bathroom. She opened the door for Sompa quickly and came to stand outside beside her.

The lights were out on the corridor so it was pretty difficult to make out the two faces who were busily making out on the corridor in the full glare of nature and the society. The lady was busily kissing the guy who pressed into her and into the door. Sompa saw a couple of girls watching and snickering, some also had their mobile phones out to catch the scene. The couple seemed lost to the attention. Either they were oblivious or they just didn't seem to care and ignored the staring eyes.

"Eii, so is this why you disturbed my sleep?" Sompa asked, her arms folded.

"Yes," Reinee said, smiling shyly, "Sorry."

"It's okay."

Sompa could see why Reinee was so excited. This wasn't Senior High school anymore. There was lots of freedom here.

"Let's leave the two lovebirds to their world," Sompa said as she opened the door to get some well-deserved sleep.

CHAPTER FOUR

Friends

The alarm went off for the fifth time in room 104 and Naomi was still turning and turning in her bed.

"Don't you have class, Nao?" Wepia called, patting the dark, tall lady awake.

And that's when Naomi bolted out of the bed.

"Gosh! Why didn't you wake me up earlier?"

"You always set your shrieking alarms so freaking early but you never wake up," Wepia said non-chalantly, "I decided to teach you a lesson."

"Gosh you are so mean, I thought you were a good person."

"Then clearly you don't really know who I am, I will discipline you."

"*Geddadehere.*"

Naomi was pissed at Wepia. She was one Moslem who removed her hijab as soon as she stepped on campus. And Nao wished that Wepia's father will suddenly knock on their door to see the kind of life his daughter was living. She looked at Tara's bed which was just opposite hers. Of course, even unserious Tara was already out for class. She was extremely late for Dr. Addo's lecture again. She hadn't even taken her bath or brushed her teeth. She hurriedly took her brush, towel and sponge and rushed to the bathroom which the whole floor shared. She didn't mind the people who stared at her in the corridor.

She all as much as threw the water on her body and dressed up before finally bolting out of the door. She headed to the faculty area and found the class that she was supposed to enter but the lecturer was already there teaching.

Immediately he turned to the whiteboard to write something down, Elikem who was seated in the front row signaled for her to come sit beside him. He had a chair for his bag and quickly removed it.

"I can't," she mouthed. She was scared that the lecturer will catch her midway into her trip and order her out of the class. She couldn't risk the embarrassment; she had a reputation to protect.

"Come, come come," he mouthed back.

When she had finally gathered enough courage to go, Naomi walked hurriedly in a squat-walk like form and quietly sat down. The lecturer turned at the right moment and continued with the lecture. She turned to Elikem and whispered, "Thank you" with a small smile.

She knew who Elikem was; she had laughed at him the first day he had stepped on campus with his chopbox, and here he was helping her. She removed her book and settled down as she tried to clean the sweat that threatened to come down her wig.

"Hello guys, I'm happy to welcome you all to your class. I'm Steven and I'm the Sociology

Students Christian Fellowship president. I'm in third year and I just want to share a word with you before your lecturer comes in. Let's all pray."

As soon as Steven finished his prayer, he began, "Yes today, I want to share my quiet time with you it is from Romans 12:1. The Lord said we should keep our bodies holy unto God. What does being Holy mean? It means being set apart for God. In Philippians 4:8, Paul admonishes us that whatever is true, whatever is noble, whatever is right, whatever is pure, whatever is lovely, whatever is admirable – if anything is excellent or praiseworthy, we should think about such things…"

Suddenly, a lady who was an hour late to the class, strutted in almost naked. She wore a very short skirt with all her thighs showing and bright nails in different colours. Her makeup was also loud; glittery eye shadow highlighted her artificial eyelashes and she wore brown contacts that were a far cry from her skin colour.

She walked in slowly and intentionally made noise with her high heels; knowing fully well that she was distracting Steven who clad his Bible tightly.

After some minutes of watching her after she had found her seat, Steven went back to the Bible preaching about how girls shouldn't wear makeup and paint their nails and how wearing short things could lead people to temptation and will lead you to hell, clearly indirectly referring to the girl who had just walked in.

Sompa cringed for the new girl as he went on, "In the last days, people will be lovers of themselves, lovers of money……Please let us not bring Sodom and Gomorrah back here again. I hope that we will all dress…"

She glanced at the new girl who had popped some two huge gums into her mouth and was busily blowing gum balloons and popping them swag style in his face. Clearly, Steven wasn't comfortable as he didn't seem to take his eyes off her cleavage.

"Please the ladies don't dress like that, it is a huge distraction and can lead to rape. You didn't come here to be a fashion queen or a slay queen.

Keep your bodies holy."

"Yeah yeah, stop addressing the women; the young guys should also keep their eyes off the ladies and keep themselves holy. Like you should be doing," she blurted out, shocking almost everyone in the room.

This shut Steven up and he had an embarrassed look on his face. After a word of prayer, Steven walked out the door with his head bowed. He had met his meter. The lady had shocked him just like she had shocked everyone else in the class.

Professor Mensah's arrival seemed to be the only thing that eased the tension in the classroom. He looked a hundred years old with white hair and amused eyes that hid behind his old-school glasses. He walked in confidently and when he spoke, he sounded like Morgan Freeman. The man who usually played the role of God in movies, at least to Sompa that's how he sounded.

"Goodmorning students, I'm Professor Mensah; you can call me Prof Mens and before we begin our first lecture, let me spell out the list of rules in this class. I detest tardiness, I detest –"

Someone had her hands up already.

"Yes, what's the problem?"

"Sir, please what is the meaning of tardiness?"

"Which SHS did you go to?"

"Sir, please I attended Royal New Drobo SHS."

"Herh, Rɔ ne Dross!" one guy at the back shouted and the whole class roared with laughter.

"Ooh no wonder," he said, throwing most of the students into fits of giggles, "Someone should please explain what tardiness means to this damsel in distress after class and don't put your SHS English teachers to shame."

"Now let me go on with my rules. I detest people sleeping in the class. In my class yawning is a crime."

"Sir, is breathing too a crime?" One boy seated at the back asked as students giggled. Some were actually shocked he had asked that question and they waited for the lecturer's reaction.

"Boy in pink who just asked that cheeky

question 'cause he's got a lot of cheeks, do not tempt me to put the fear of God into you," he boomed, "The next time, you will be out of my class for the rest of the semester. YOU HEAR?"

"Y-y-yes Sir," he mumbled.

"Good. And to you all, if you miss my class more than three times, you will not write my exams. I hope I have made myself clear."

The tension in the room was back as his teaching assistant, a cute girl with dark skin walked in with sheets of paper. Sompa wondered how she was able to work with such an irate man. She was sure that if this man ever asked her a question in class, she would pee on herself.

"The papers that are being passed to you now are what we will be reading in class today. That should be your mantra for this programme. Now I want someone to read it to the whole class."

He scanned the whole class, his eyes deftly settling on the lady who was busy blowing bubble gums and popping them with her mouth.

"Yes the lady in red, stand up and read aloud."

The lady stood up disinterested and walked to

the front of the class, showing off her curves and really thick thighs and super high heels. Her attitude seemed to get Prof Mens incensed.

"Young lady, did you come here to tempt us? Were you sent by the devil? Why are you wearing such dresses?" He asked, "Go and change. I'm not allowing you to distract us. Come on, get out of my class."

"But Sir, what is wrong with my dress? I just arrived from America today."

"I don't care whether you arrived from Mars, go and change and I will not repeat myself again."

"No Sir I won't leave, after all I paid my school fees."

"Eii this girl no dey fear." Sompa heard some of the guys murmuring at the back.

"What? Did you just say that to me? I want you out of my class now." He said in a loud voice which pretty much scared her off. She rolled her eyes in annoyance, walked over to her seat to take her bag and modelled out of the door, deliberately blowing and popping the gum as she did so.

"Such insolence!" he said shaking his head,

"Please wear decent dresses when attending lectures…It's in your Student Guide. Ah well, more than half of you do not even read. Why should I waste my breath? Yes, I need a volunteer."

But the class had gone quiet. No one dared raise his or her hand.

"Anyone? No one? Fine. Then your first assignment…" Everyone groaned at the mention of the assignment, "Your first assignment is to appreciate the poem. It should be at least two pages, text should be in Times New Roman, twelve points. It should be submitted with a cover page."

No one was happy with this not even Sompa who knew that she will not be able to enjoy her weekend properly with this assignment looming over her.

After attending another class in the afternoon that ended at 4pm, Sompa took her bag after giving a rushed hello to her friend and coursemate, Elise and headed for her dormitory. She yearned for her bed. But she decided to pass through Aban Hall which was known for their famous hot yam chips and pork, chicken and gizzard khebab.

She hurried to the porters Lodge for her key but was informed that someone had already come for it. *Renee must be in the room*, she thought as she walked briskly and turned to the corridor where her room was located.

"Who do you think you are?!" a girl screamed angrily at another in the corridor.

People had gathered at the scene and Sompa feared that by walking through the fight she might be roped in.

"Leave Kwadwo alone, he is mine!!!" the other girl retorted.

"I will slap you back to the country you came from."

"Try, I'll beat you first."

That seemed to get the other girl incensed and they lunged for each other. Wigs flew in the air.

"What's happening here? Who are those girls?" she asked one of the onlookers.

"You remember the lady who was kissing the

guy one night? Apparently the guy already had a girlfriend and now the side chick and the main chick are fighting over him; who knows there might be more."

"Hmm, side dishes and main dishes, let me find some other place to pass."

Already outside, the clouds had started to gather and it looked like it was going to rain heavily. She passed the East Wing to her room and knocked on the door.

"I'm coming…" the unfamiliar voice called and she wondered who it could possibly be.

The door opened. Sompa couldn't believe it was her.

CHAPTER FIVE

Daddies

"What are you doing in my room?"

"Nice to meet you too," she said with a smile that didn't reach her eyes as she deliberately popped a bubble gum in her face. It was the same girl with the giant attitude she had seen in class. "Hi, I'm Dorcas and I am your third roommate."

"Okay, I'm Sompa," she replied, consciously leaving out the 'nice to meet you'. She was still shocked. She didn't like her. It wasn't nice to meet her. She hurried in just as she heard thunder strike nearby. Her being here was certainly a bad omen of some sort.

Dorcas shut the door and continued with the storm she was brewing in the room. Her clothes were everywhere as she unpacked. She took the down bed and quickly laid her bed.

Sompa settled in her bed and ate her yam and pork as she watched her with interest. She danced to some hip-hop on her phone.

Her clothes, shoes and bags were so many that Sompa almost thought that she came to pursue another course in Slaying because no books were in sight. And it looked like she had brought the whole house with her.

After Dorcas was done packing which had filled her part of the wardrobe, she signaled Sompa.

"Umm Sompa, I have something to tell you…just so we are clear, I have a serious schedule of Daddies."

"Daddy?"

"Umm yeah, Sugar Daddies, I have one that comes every Friday, one that comes on Mondays and one who will be coming on Sundays. I just wanted you to know so that it doesn't become confusing when I am switching between men, ok and keep this to yourself, ok?"

"You switch between men? What about

STDs? Are you not scared?"

"No, I protect myself," Dorcas said, amused that she was concerned about her.

Sompa made a mental note to be careful around Dorcas. "Okay, you have to tell the other girl too when she gets back. She's called Renee."

"Alright, and since we are doing the same course, I could give you a lift sometimes."

"Thank you but I'm sure I'll be fine." Sompa obviously did not want to benefit from Dorcas' Sugar and Daddies.

Dorcas shrugged, "Alright, suit yourself."

Dorcas didn't care what Sompa thought of her. It was better if people knew her for who she was than to pretend and surprise them later. The world will be a much better place if people were upfront about who they were. With her revelation and efforts, she meant to reduce the number of fake people in the world. That trip to America was awesome. She had travelled on the arm and sponsorship of Sir Daddy who was very much married but who liked to have fun with her sometimes. She enjoyed his pampering so much and he had promised her she could pick a country for their next vacation and this had left her elated. She had used his credit card to buy so many bags, shoes and clothes. She hoped to start her own boutique with the clothes now that she was on campus.

"My baby really loves to be spoiled," he said the night she had come to the hotel with a spree of all America.

She settled down on her bed as she filed her nails; satisfied that she could finally start her journey. Finally she was here! The university of her dreams; pursuing the course she loved all from her hard-earned money. No family had supported her. Not even her parents; her parents who had brought her into the world to come and suffer. Her father had shown her very well at a young age that she could get anywhere with what God had endowed her with. She didn't even know what a real daddy felt like. She was certainly not going back to that village. Mahatma Gandhi was right, poverty was indeed violence. Never again was she going to beg; never again was she going to lower her gaze, never again was she going to let opportunities that were meant for her pass her by.

––––––––––––––––––––––––––

Araba stared at the new roommate who had just arrived. Racheal was out as usual; she barely even saw her unless she had another class during the day. Her name was Maame and she was friendly, and just like Araba feared she was a Jesus Freak. God hadn't listened to her just like he always hadn't. She looked so happy to be in the University and Araba guessed that Maame was a serious *dadabee* as she watched them chat in the room. Her parents helped her to unpack as they listened to her ramble on about how she had read Psalm 64 this morning and how she was so sure that she was destined for the room.

"You know how much I have prayed about this room, Mummy?"

"Yes my daughter, and I know you'll make us proud," her mother smiled at her and gave her a deep hug.

Araba rolled her eyes and put the earpiece on to listen to Simi's *Original Baby* to drown out the beautiful camaraderie. She couldn't help but feel a little jealous. One year ago, this would have been her with her mum and dad but Essaba's leaving had left the family broken. Her mummy had never been the same again. Everyday staring into her mother's empty bloodshot eyes was torture for her. Her mother barely did anything around the house. She barely even slept. Every night, Daddy had to fill her drink with sleeping pills so that at least she could have some rest. Every morning, she would rinse her mouth with alcohol. At least the bottle offered some momentary numbness and forgetfulness where she could not feel the pain anymore.

She closed her eyes and pushed the memory of Esaaba's smiling face aside. Just then Joey called and she picked.

"Hey, what's up? I know I promised to take you on a tour of the school and now this is the time to make good on that promise. Are you free this evening?"

"Yeah I am, I would definitely want to come," she replied. She was up for anything that will take her mind off her big sister.

"Great, then I will come by around 4."

"See you."

_____

The two of them walked under the stars after getting an ice cream and passing through the Osagyefo Hall. Joey had an affiliation to that hall and he recounted some of the funny encounters he had had.

"Hahahaha, so did you ever join the jama group anytime they went out to charge?"

"I must admit, I joined them once when I was in first year and didn't know anything. I think it must have been my mum's prayers that saved me because during that moment, it was like something just entered me."

"Woow really?" she laughed.

"Yes, it's that time that you get to see even the most gentlest of guys become different people. I think the tradition of the hall is more than meets the eye. It has a lot of spiritual connotations."

"That's scary, with this story, I'm not sure I will ever enter that hall."

"Oh don't worry, just don't pass there when they are having their hall week or when they charge. You wouldn't want to see guys drinking and almost naked, some kraa sometimes dress like women with wigs."

"Eeish that must be something." They neared towards the library where they sat down to finish their cups of ice cream.

"This is the Hughes Hall. This is where the busts of past Vice Chancellors are. You can look at their names. And this is where most important ceremonies like public lectures and speeches are held in the University," Joey said gesturing to all the heads. Araba went round the various busts taking note of the names. She wondered how the Vice Chancellors were when they had been living.

Joey had shown her around the administration offices, the East-West Mall, the commercial area, the gardens and the pool side. He was yet to show her the various social centres in the school.

Joey enjoyed Araba's company. She was so easy. This year's October Rush was going to be lit. Who knew he will at least score one nil before leaving the four walls of the University. He too his time had come.

He stared at their empty cups and into her eyes. For a moment, he was lost in her big browns and Araba warmed up to his gaze. He was so handsome.

"My friend will be having his birthday drink up this evening, will you like to come be my plus one," he spoke in a tone that she couldn't resist.

"Sure." She liked this. She liked him. They held hands as they walked.

They headed for the Ectasy Club which was nothing like Araba had ever been to. People were serious on the dance floor, some were drinking and others were making conversation. The disco lights danced emphatically, highlighting the mood of the place.

"Wow," she said looking around. She had never been to a night bar before and immediately she felt like a fish out of water.

"Yeah wow! You are going to have fun here tonight," Joey whispered into her ears away from the loud music, "Let me get you a drink."

After disappearing into the crowd for a few minutes, Joey came back with two cups of wine and lemon. The liquid looked so transparent and harmless and Araba downed it quickly. She liked the small burn it left as it travelled down her throat. She wanted another.

"I need another," she said.

"More drinks please," he called as he led her to sit down on the bar stool.

After the waiter served them with more drinks, Araba could hear her phone ring again.

"Won't you pick it up? It's been ringing since we started this tour."

She stared at the number although she already knew who was calling.

"I won't. Let's go and dance now." Too much wine meant that she needed to dance it off. She pulled Joey to the dance floor and danced to some music. Joey could tell that she was drunk already but didn't care as he planted a kiss on her lips. She didn't stop him. She liked it. He made her forget all her problems.

CHAPTER SIX

Margaret Thatcher

"Nao, I'm craving Adjoa *Gobɛ* o. I want *gobɛ* and the whole works – sausages, egg and pear with a lot of *zomi*. Do you think she came today?" Sompa asked as she felt her stomach grumble. They had been studying for so many hours obviously nearing their Mid-Semester Exams which was going to start in two weeks and neither of them had had the time to cook anything. Plus there was *dumsor* and unfortunately their stoves couldn't run on air.

They had spent so many hours in the study room/library studying. As for her roommate, Dorcas, she hadn't even seen her open her books. Nothing moved that girl.

"Of course she comes everyday even on

Sundays. She knows she's really the student's saviour. Her *Gobɛ* has really changed lives and motivated people la. Let's go."

"Eii those Broad way Boys."

"Let's go…I'm in no mood for their snide comments," Nao encouraged.

They left their books in the room and walked out into the sun confidently.

"Chaii, who angered the sun today. It is too hot," Sompa remarked.

"Let's get that Gobɛ, we will be back in no time," Naomi urged as they neared the Broad Way where Adwoa Gobɛ's stand was right behind Central Hall Annex.

There was a huge queue there. It was made up of mostly guys who were ordering their afternoon dose of Adwoa Gobɛ. There were a few brave girls there like Naomi and Sompa who were in the queue. Everything seemed to be moving on smoothly until someone decided to shout.

"Girl in the green dress, the breast is it for only you?"

"It is for me and your mother!" Naomi

retorted. That shut the boy up as the other guys snickered and jeered at him.

"Eii you are combining eggs, sausages and *Gobε*. Your roommates will suffer o."

"And you will too!" She replied as the guys laughed at the guy who had dared open his mouth. Nao was really prepared for them. To her, she felt like she was fighting for the whole generation of women. She hated how the guys made them feel like they weren't marriage material when they were found queuing for food.

"Nao, waow, what got into you, I'm even shy and proud to be walking with you mpo," Sompa remarked as she held tightly to their orders.

"I told you I was ready for them and I was. I won't allow them to say crap to my face and go scot free. *Hwε*," Nao said, "I'm going to eat my *gobε* in peace."

"Naomi," someone called.

"Yes," she turned and saw Elikem walking briskly towards them.

"Who's that?"

"That's Elikem, the chopbox boy," she

whispered.

"Hello," he smiled shyly as his forehead glistened in the sun.

"Hi."

"That was some show back there," he praised.

"Oh so you were there?" Nao asked suddenly shy which made Sompa wonder why.

"Yes I saw everything, Margaret Thatcher," he teased.

"Oh *gyae me*," Nao said smiling, "Someone had to shut their mouths."

"And that someone had to be you."

"Yes, my mother would have been disappointed in me if I hadn't," she remarked.

"Well I'm glad, you made me laugh today." He asked, "How are studies going?"

"IImm, I still don't get some stuff under Anatomy and Physiology and Pharmaceutics (Dispensing)."

"I could help you if you don't mind and I have got some past questions too. So we can meet later today at the Aban Study room."

"Okay, thank you. Oh hey, this is my friend,

Sompa," Naomi informed, "Sompa, this is Elikem."

"I know right; the one and only chopbox boy," he said, extending his palm.

"Hahahaa, don't worry everyone will forget soon," Sompa said sweetly, "I'm honoured to meet you."

"Pleased to meet you too."

"Thanks Elikem so I will see you at 4pm."

"Sure."

When Elikem was out of sight, Sompa quipped, "Somebody likes somebody o. You've got yourself an admirer. He likes you."

"Oh how do you know?"

"The way he was smiling and looking at you, it's like there was some light bi in his eyes."

"He's a nice guy fine. I don't even mind that he brought a chopbox to school but-"

"But you like him too…"

"No I don't."

"Ooh you so do, I feel like I have known you forever. You so like him."

"I don't, stop the fooling; you are making me

lose appetite for the gobε."

"Only love makes you lose appetite for food, my dear."

"Oh gyae me."

"Margaret Thatcher has fallen hard."

———————————————

After Naomi had left for the study meeting with Elikem, Sompa settled to do some more reading before she dozed off. None of her roomies were around and she decided to get as much of personal study time. Renee was probably sleeping at her boyfriend's place. He had a whole room to himself so she was free to perch there. At first she didn't understand why Renee seemed to disappear for hours on end and then she soon understood why when she later introduced her boyfriend to her.

Well, she was glad, because it meant that Renee hardly used her fridge. Renee was the only one who had brought a fridge and a television and living on campus for almost four weeks, Sompa began to appreciate how essential the fridge was. Especially when it came to preserving her foods. It was hard enough cooking on an electric stove but more difficult using conventional means to preserve the food. She had to cook in small amounts because if she cooked a lot, the stew or soup will go stale after too much heating and all the nutrients in the food will be lost. In the beginning, Renee had been very selfish about her fridge and didn't want any of them to use it. It never even bothered Dorcas as she hardly cooked in the room. She usually bought or ate outside. But as the weeks passed by, Renee began to allow Sompa to keep her foods in the fridge so long as she kept the fridge clean.

And as for Dorcas, her schedule was on. That girl hardly opened her books to study and most of the time she was out. She always came back to the room late. Sompa hated that she always disturbed her sleep so one night, she told her that she should get a copy of the key for herself because she couldn't keep opening doors for her else she was going to lock her out one of these nights.

Dorcas was partly surprised and glad that Sompa scolded her like that. She had always thought that she was quiet. Now she knew she had personality. *Good, I've set the spark,* she thought and went to have the copy done. Sompa had wondered how calm Dorcas was in the face of exams. *Perhaps she's studying and I don't know,* she thought.

After staring at the mountain of books on her bed for two hours, she decided it was time to take a nap as she felt a headache threatening to break out behind her eyes.

She pushed the books aside and set her alarm. With exams nearing, she needed as much time to study. But right now she needed some sleep.

It must have been minutes, maybe hours when Sompa heard a knock on the door. It woke her up from her short reverie and she grudgingly rolled off the top bed and went down to open the door.

"Is she here?" the tall old man who wore dark glasses was fuming.

"Who are you? And who are you looking for please?" She was partly annoyed.

"I'm looking for Renee. I hear she is in this room."

"Yes she is but she is not here at the moment."

"That girl eh, if I get her –"

"Please should I leave a message for you?"

"No, no don't bother."

"Well, what's your name so that I tell her that you came by?"

"No, no don't tell her I came by. This meeting never happened you hear?"

"Umm okay." She wondered why this weird old man didn't want her to know but she decided to tell her, when she came around the following weekend to change her clothes. Dorcas was there failing at attempts to read her book and she had given up to some series on her laptop.

Sompa saw Renee holding an iPhone.

"Nice phone, don't think I've seen it around before."

"Why? Are you supposed to know about every part of my life?"

"I'm sorry. Renee, someone came looking for you, I think on Tuesday."

"Really who was it?"

"An old man, he was really mad. Do you know who it was or have you offended someone recently?"

"I dunno." But looking at her eyes, Sompa could tell that she knew who it was.

"Did he tell you his name?"

"No. Was it your father?"

"No, my father died a long time ago."

"Oh," Sompa didn't know what to say.

"Well, next time he comes here, tell him I don't live here anymore, ok?"

"Ook."

———————————

Steven didn't understand why he couldn't get her out of his head. Was he just obsessed with her? Was he falling in love with her? He couldn't tell and yet she wasn't his kind of girl. When he usually thought about his beloved, he imagined a quiet beautiful girl who dressed decently and had the fear of God in her not this girl with the attitude and loud personality.

Ever since she had made the comment while he had been preaching, she had been impressed upon his heart and mind. He couldn't shake off thoughts of her and wondered if the devil was playing with his mind.

Every time she came up in his thoughts, he would mutter to himself, "Flee, Flee." But it didn't seem to work. He had even spent two weeks at Fawohodie Park to pray about the issue but ha! The devil was a liar. Nothing seemed to be working. Until he had a weird dream about her. In the dream, he had seen her without the paint she usually wore and she had come to see him. It had felt natural that she had come to visit him and she had brought along some food. He had tasted her food and it had been so good in the dream. When he woke up, he knew what it meant. He watched her with keen interest as she walked around in the faculty. He always saw her chewing her gum and carrying her books, always spotted in something short.

He began to like her because she intrigued him

and he felt God was telling him that this was his future wife. He felt that God was telling him to date her and change her. He didn't know how to approach as he was scared that she would embarrass him like she did the other time. The following day, he decided to shoot his shot when he saw her speaking to her lecturer. He waited for her to finish and came out to meet her.

"Hello, I am Steven." She looked at him from the top of his head to the sole of his feet as if she wondered why a guy of his caliber will approach her.

"Yes, what do you want?" She was impatient. She immediately recognized him as the guy who had subtly preached against her on her first day.

Steven was caught off guard. He knew she was rude but didn't expect that she will be this rude to him.

"Oh I just want to be your friend," he protested. "What is your name?"

"My name is Dorcas."

"Ooh like the blessed Dorcas in the Bible."

"No, I think I am more like Jezebel who tried

to kill the vineyard man and scare Elijah, you know oh and the one who cut off Samson's locks. What was her name again, yes Delilah," she said with confidence in an attempt to scare him off. She only intrigued him more.

He sighed. *At least she knows who those two women are in the Bible*, he comforted himself with that thought as he pressed on.

"I'm in third year, so I just want you to know that if you need help with any of the courses I am right here."

"Thank you. You are too kind, but I won't be needing your help. I am not struggling with my studies." Her artificial nails gleamed in the sunlight.

"Ok but can we become friends or hopefully more than friends? We could hang out sometime." Why didn't she see this coming? His smile was showing off his thirty-two teeth which reminded her of the piranha fish she had seen at the aquarium or the fish that Ghanaians lovingly called Ewura Efua.

"Why would you want to date someone like

me? Upon all the church girls and the prayer partners you have, why me?"

"I like you."

"You like me? Are you sure you like me? I am not a virgin and I don't wear dresses that flow from Kumasi to Accra like your church girlfriends. I don't believe in God. He failed me so I'm not getting into bed with Him again," she informed him calmly.

"Don't worry Dorcas, he has not given up on you. Who knows you might change."

"And when we become more than friends where will we go on dates. The Fawohodie Park to pray or what?"

"Oh we could go out to get some pizza and coke, or some Kofi Brokeman kraa or some *Gobɛ* you know?"

"I am sorry, Steven. I don't waste my time like that. I don't do pizza and coke boys or fried rice and chicken. I am not enthralled by those 45 and 50 Ghana cedis meals and sitting in the taxi whiles I listen to your boring Christian prayerful jokes. For dates, I go to places that you can only dream about and eat foods that both of us cannot even pronounce. The world is more than just roasted plantain groundnuts and beans and bread and cheese and fizzy drinks," she said and sauntered off deliberately shaking her hips, letting him know that he couldn't afford her.

"Ooh YAWA O Yawaaa!" Steven shook his head as he watched her walk away. He was just glad that he hadn't told any of his friends that he was going to ask her out else they would have watched and laughed at his embarrassment.

At least God for your kingdom I tried, he comforted himself with that thought.

As he passed by the group of boys who suddenly exploded with laughter, he felt like they were mocking him. She had ruined his day.

Dorcas couldn't believe he had the guts to even approach her. He couldn't even afford her. *Mtcccchew such a nuisance,* she thought. A guy who couldn't spread her and live up to her expensive tastes and high standards, was that one too a boyfriend? Poverty wasn't her portion.

CHAPTER SEVEN

Shatta anointing

"Araba, Araba, wake up it's time for church."

Araba moaned in her sleep and turned the other way.

"Araba, Araba." Now the voice was really getting on her nerves.

"Oh what is it?" she asked in annoyance as she felt a wave of pain and nausea throughout her whole body. Who told her to wear those heels and drink that much last night?

"Esther said I shouldn't leave you this time. She's been calling you the whole of two months! We attend the same church remember?"

"Who is Esther? Is she my mother?"

"She's …" and she stopped when she realized Araba was just being sarcastic.

"I can't get up. Just go without me."

"No I won't."

Now Araba knew that God really didn't listen to her prayers when she asked for no Jesus freaks to be her roommate. Come to think of it, where was her other roommate?

"Then be there, because I am not moving an inch from this bed. You know I came home late from a night out with Joey so don't come and worry me about church. On the seventh day God rested and that's just what I'm doing."

"Joey is not helping you."

"Maame, I don't need a mother here ok? That's why I came all the way here to be far away from my parents as possible."

"Please, what will be preached today may be just what you might need to hear."

"I don't care. My sleep is more important. If you won't leave then stand there. I won't be held responsible for not allowing you to go to church."

She turned away and clucked with annoyance. She waited for some few minutes until she heard the door shut.

"Church too, is it by force?" she muttered. "No one should come and disturb my peace here."

After some few minutes she couldn't help but feel sorry for the way she had acted towards Maame. After all, she was doing her angelic duty of making sure she didn't miss heaven. It was the headache and this great hangover. Joey and his kisses and the wine offered some momentary amnesia which numbed the pain. *How do those who party frequently do this?* She wondered and took account of her life. Some years ago she would not have done this and having to wake up from the weekend from a hangover every single time. What was she turning into? She was really turning into someone she didn't like right now. Her mother and the bottles came to mind and with that disturbing thought, she went back to sleep.

A few minutes later, Maame met Esther.

"Where is she?"

"She doesn't want to come. She said we should stop bothering her."

"Well…we may stop asking her to come but we are not giving up on her," she said determinedly, "Let's pray for her."

And they both bowed their heads and closed their eyes as they prayed silently.

There was something so beautiful and chilly about early Sunday mornings at church. It wasn't just the praise and worship or the sound of the trumpets, no it was the atmosphere. Noisy on the outside but calm and solemn on the inside.

Sompa moved as the choir sang, "He's able." And led through the solo. Today, there was a new guitar guy and he played so well. Sompa could feel his eyes on her throughout the service. The topic for the service was 'The man who has' but only God knew she wasn't paying much attention. The guitar guy unashamedly stared at her and she stared back.

It was therefore no surprise that after the service he approached her before she could leave. He was of average height and he had eyes that were full with his eyebrows and long eyelashes.

His eyes were the kind that smiled kindly.

"Hi, I'm Percy. What's your name?"

"I'm Sompa. Never seen you around before."

"That's because I joined the church just this week."

"Ok that's great. I hope you'll stay."

"Yeah, you've got such a lovely voice why can't I stay?" At this, Sompa's smile flashed. "We could do a duo sometime with my acoustic guitar."

"Really? I would love to."

"Great, so we could be meeting every Wednesdays."

"Okay sure, let's just have the midsems pass please. Two weeks pɛ," she said with a smile.

"Alright, I'll see you around."

———————————————

God was good! God had indeed blessed her with this body to be sharing! This is what she needed every Sunday. It felt like her body was made up of nerve-endings. His hand explored her breasts as she moved on him rhythmically filling her with sensations. But to her they were just sensations. They meant nothing to her.

"Climax!" he screamed as she felt his release. His sweat cascaded down his protruded belly as he breathed fast and heavily. One thing she didn't like about sleeping with old men was that their waists were too weak and they could last a few seconds but this man! He had the stamina of a young man.

He liked the sight of her long hot pink acrylic nails that dug into his skin and her perfume that was full of berries and vanilla. She was definitely so much better than his wife who was a nun when it came to sex. His wife had never felt the need to jazz up their sex life; always wanting it one way and with the lights off. He listened to Shatta Wale's *Hol' it* song that played on the speakers. This lovely vixen on top of him was the one who had put in the song.

"Wow, you are so amazing. If you could keep this up, I will give you all As in your assignments and exams and you wouldn't even have to work for it." He smiled appreciatively at her. This was definitely a great way to spend the Sabbath.

"Yes Sir, I'll continue to give you the Shatta anointing every Sunday so long as you keep your end of the bargain."

"I like when you talk dirty. I told you to drop the 'Sir' title though."

She giggled, "It's dirtier and naughtier when I call you sir," she continued, "Make sure your Teaching Assistant doesn't become suspicious."

"I will make sure. Come and give me some good loving for your punishment. The little guy is up again, come and let's put him to rest."

They kissed and fondled and cuddled and when they were done, he reached out for a cuddle but she stood up from the bed.

"Please stay." He reached for her hand but she pulled his away.

"You know I never stay. That's my policy."

"I've always known you to be a rule breaker."

"Yeah, yeah but I don't break my own rules."

"Do you have other people you sleep with?" He blurted out after a moment. Because the thought of her serving the town didn't look good to him. He never liked to share.

"And what is it to you? Just mind your business and fulfill your end of the bargain." With that he knew he was definitely sharing her. He watched her as she quickly pulled on her clothes and freshened up and combed out her purple wig. He watched her through the big mirror and saw those brave brown eyes staring back.

He couldn't help but wonder who could have made her this way. She was the same age as his daughter. Who had crossed her path?

"I'm leaving," she kissed his forehead one last time and headed for the door.

"Wait, let me take you to your hostel."

"No thank you, I would be fine. Just remember that I am with you but I am not yours."

Dorcas didn't care that her lecturer, who was the Head of Department was trying to be considerate. He was a predator just like her father.

She remembered the day he had called her to wait for him after class. She remembered how he had looked down on her from his glasses taking note of her breasts and her waist and the skirt that wasn't longer than a tennis skirt which showed off her fair fresh thighs and legs. She recalled the small office and wondered if those rumours happened in the room.

"Yes, Dorcas…I have closely watched you and it's unfortunate to know that you are already falling behind with your work."

"What can be done?" she asked already knowing what he was going to offer her.

"You can either make sure that you get 90 in the upcoming exams or I could take you on a flight with my leg."

Nevertheless, she was still surprised that he would ask her to do that. Wasn't he married? Didn't he have children? Wasn't he a family man? Didn't he love his wife? Often when the men made such offers, she wondered what drove them to make such decisions.

"Why do you look surprised or you are not interested in men?"

She was just surprised and amused that he put his request that way.

"Ah Sir, why would I go for oranges when there are bananas?" she asked, making sure that he got a good view of her.

"Good so we meet on Sunday."

"What time?"

"4pm."

And here she was. It had been so long since she had picked up a book to study and it was difficult finding concentration. This was the only way out. Her body.

CHAPTER EIGHT

Caught by surprise

Nao woke up to her shrilling phone and smiled when she saw the caller.

"*Sore, sore na wa da kakraa eye.*" He sounded like a shrieking siren.

"Oh Eli let me sleep small, eh?"

"Are you up or you are just changing gears?"

"I'm up now, Eli."

"Are you sure you won't ask me later if I called you in your dreams."

"Oh Eli stop worrying me. I know I have a sleeping problem. Just thank God that I actually heard your call and picked," she said with laughter in her voice.

"Good and glad I managed to be an alarm that actually wakes you up today," his warm voice came through the phone, "It's Midsem break and I'll be taking you out so get prepared dear."

"Alright Eli, you sound so excited and mischievous. Only God knows what you have up your sleeve."

"That's for me to know and for you to find out. So I will meet you soon."

"Sure Eli, see you soon."

The one week of the Mid semester exams went by very well. Well…for some students who studied hard. It was a great relief when it was finally over and classes were back into full session. The students also looked forward to the various hall week celebrations that were coming up.

Naomi, Elikem and Sompa spent most of the time attending programmes, watching the various hall week celebrations. Three things most people enjoyed about the hall week celebrations was the music, the noise and the many food joints that were set up at the various halls. The trio never missed out on an evening of khebab and lots of powdered pepper with kelewele.

But at some point Sompa had to leave the two lovebirds and attend her Wednesday meetings with Percy.

―――――――――――――――――

He was such a good friend and Sompa enjoyed his company. She got to know a lot more about him. He did Medicine but loved music so much that he spent most of his time pursuing it. She got to know how his perspective on life had changed after he had puked whiles dissecting a frog and a cadaver. He hadn't liked the sight of blood but had gotten so used to it that he wanted to be a surgeon. They had rehearsed so many new songs together. It was Wednesday again and they were in his room.

"Let's take the song again," he said as he sat on the swivel chair beside her with his guitar. "This time let's record."

"Alright." She pulled out her phone and opened the recorder app as Percy struck his guitar.

She closed her eyes and let the song flow from

her lips

Hello my friend

I remember when you were

So alive, with your wide eyes then the light

that you had in your heart was stolen

Now you say that it aint worth staying

You wanna run but you're hesitating

I'm talking to me

Don't let your lights go down

Don't let your fire burn out

Cos somewhere somebody needs a reason to believe

Why don't you rise up now.

Don't be afraid to stand out

That's how the lost get found.

"That's amazing. Now let's listen to the recording," Percy said after the song ended.

"That was great. Britt Nicole will be proud." He smiled at her throughout as the song came to an end.

"Yes, you played the chords very well, pal." She smiled back.

There was a long moment as he put down his

guitar and did something that she hadn't seen coming. He kissed her. She was so surprised and partly angry that he had done that suddenly. She tried to get away but he pulled her back and kissed her some more. And this time she didn't pull away. Her defenses were weakening and her walls of Jericho were coming down fast. She kissed back and she knew he knew what he was doing to her.

She pulled back and bit her lip with regret as she looked at him. He looked like he really enjoyed it and smirked as he stared at her.

"Why did you do that?" She was angrier that he had stolen her first kiss.

"Because I really needed to. And I know you enjoyed it too."

"Yeah, you know that was my first kiss."

"Oh really? Didn't know you have never been kissed before."

"Gosh! What got into you?! You know we are Christians and we just committed fornication."

"Gosh Sompa, don't get so worked up it was just a kiss."

"Apparently, it wasn't just a kiss to me. I am

never coming here again. This is the last time."

He didn't say anything but watched as she picked up her bag and left the room. She was so shattered. And to think that all those plans in her diary could be thrown out the window just like that. She hurriedly left and didn't stop even though it was raining. She remembered the purity vow she had taken at the youth camp back at home some two years ago. She remembered how she had repeated those words earnestly and with integrity. She remembered how much she wanted to take a stand for God, especially in this modern era when everything seemed to be alright and everything had rights. She was glad that the rain that came down her face masked her teary heart. Never again.

As soon as she got to her room, she made a sign of the cross and asked God for forgiveness.

Araba and Joey were having the time of their lives. They always went out and came back very late. Maame was really sad as she recalled how much she had been looking forward to making new friends with her roommates. Maame was always holed up in the room studying or watching a movie. The only other place apart from class that she was interested in was church. From church, back to the room. Unless there was a special programme at church. She had really enjoyed the annual church socialization and date night. That day she got to play some football with the guys. And later that night, she got to wear a really pretty ash dress with a shiny brooch and some beautiful silver shoes that her mother got for her. Even that day Ekow smiled at her like she was the most beautiful lady in the world. She had never felt so alive like that day. Running around, heart beating, sweat trickling, and feeling strong she thanked God she felt no pain. Feeling healthy was something that she was never going to take for granted.

Breathing came easier to her now and she didn't have to carry that bag around. The other girl hardly stayed over because her house was in the same city as the University. The hall week celebration at the Central Hall which was the celebration that everyone seemed to be looking forward to was the biggest and baddest of all hall week celebrations. It was heaven to the people who enjoyed it and hell's annex to most 'Chrife' people. The drinks, the booze, the various food joints, the smoke and the people really made it look like one. This year, artistes like King Promise, Shatta Wale and Patapaaa were invited. Students from various universities were also going to attend the event. It really promised to be awesome.

Araba was especially *woke* about the whole thing and picked out a dress that would fit the occasion. It barely passed her knees. Funny enough, she got a call from her dad that evening.

"How are you doing, my girl?"

"I'm okay. How are you too?

"I'm fine I was just calling to check on you since you have decided not to call ever since you stepped onto campus." He was trying to make her feel guilty but he was earnestly failing.

"Well…thank you. Is Mummy better?"

"No, she just keeps staring into the ceiling and sometimes out the windows; not saying a word. I'm very scared that one of these days she's just going to leave."

Araba went silent. At least it was better if she left. She hated how her mood spoiled the whole atmosphere of the house and once again she was glad she had Joey to escape to.

"Well…I just wanted to hear your voice. Hope you are taking care of yourself out there. Don't do what I wouldn't do."

"Okay bye." At the other end of the line, Mr. Hammond wondered why his daughter sounded so distant. She wasn't as cheerful as she used to be. Well ever since Esaaba left, nothing had been the same. It felt like his family was breaking apart.

She was gloomy one second and brightened when she received a call from Joey.

At 6:30 pm, the Central Hall was lit. This is what she came to school for. Yes, this was what she had been waiting for. Patapaa was serving them some of the hot "One Corner" song and then

King Promise came in and Shatta Wale's performance was what dragged on into the night. She danced and partied, she drank some more, she ate some khebabs, she drank again and danced again.

The party was really the littest ever. Lit enough to forget her troubles. She danced the whole night away with Joey but was unaware when Joey put something in her drink before handing it over to her. He watched and smiled diabolically as she drank it and asked for more. *This Araba girl is indeed too easy. I am going to leave my mark before I leave this school. I can proudly say that at least I scored one nil this night,* he thought as he got her another glass and poured more of the concoction in the drink. If she ever tasted it she didn't even show it. She was too drunk.

Araba began to feel a burning sensation in her abdomen and didn't understand. She wasn't aware when he took her key and led her to her room. As soon as he saw that the room was dark, he knew that Maame wasn't in there. This was his chance.

He put on his phone's flash and camera to video the scene. He turned the key in and opened the door. He removed the key but forgot to lock it and started to kiss her in the dark. He was so happy when she responded although he knew that she was not aware. He gently unhooked her bra and started to kiss her breasts. He slowly undressed her as he did so. *She is so sweet*, he thought as his mouth explored her body.

He was so much into it that he didn't hear when the door knob turned and Maame stood in the door way horrified.

She stared at the scene going on in the room and hurriedly put on the light.

"What the hell are you doing to Araba? Get out of here right this minute before I report you for rape."

Dang! He had been caught! He got off the bed and hurriedly put on his trousers and shirt.

This wasn't how it was supposed to end.

"I can explain-" he began.

"You can explain by deleting that from your phone right now. I don't care if it's the latest

IPhone. I am going to smash it on the floor." He had never thought Maame to be this dangerous. She sounded so dangerous right now.

She made sure that he deleted the video from his phone right under her nose.

"I am so-"

"Save it for her. You know clearly that she is not conscious and you are doing this? What kind of a friend are you? You guys think that we women are objects that you can use and go? I have met your kind before."

"Please don't report –"

"Just thank God that I know Him, I would have killed you right now." She was dangerously calm as she stood in the doorway.

"I don't want to see you come near her ever again, if you do I swear I shall report you to the appropriate authorities. You want to just have her and share her videos to other guys so they'll laugh and you'll be proud. How childish you are!"

He stood staring at her looking all disheveled. "You are still standing here. Get out of here!"

She heaved out a sigh when he was finally out

of the room and she stared at Araba's seemingly lifeless form on the bed. She was knocked out too much. Whatever Joey had put into her drink was really strong. She gently covered her with her blanket and hoped that she will be better by morning.

CHAPTER NINE

Revelations

"Eli, I'm dying," his mother coughed out as she spoke. He realized how croaked and hoarse his mother's voice sounded.

"What? What's wrong?" Elikem could barely get the words out. Naomi sensed that something was wrong and moved to hug him from the back. She hoped that everything was alright. This past few months had been a whirlwind and they had fallen in love with each other so much.

"I have cancer," she whispered and Elikem could sense that she was in pain.

"When did you know?"

"Two months back. I discovered a lump in my breasts…I thought it would go but it has gotten worse. I went for a breast screening and I have been diagnosed with cancer."

"Oh my God!" Eli covered his mouth with his palms.

"I didn't want to tell you. I didn't want you to worry. I'm so sorry."

"But you can beat this right?"

"It's slim but I'll take the chance."

"I hope you feel better. I will come ho-"

"No, you are not moving an inch from campus. You have to study and pursue your dreams. That is what will make me happy and feel better."

"But Mummy-"

"No Eli, I'll be fine, how is Naomi?" Elikem could sense her weak attempt to move on to other topics.

"She's doing fine."

"Great, send my greetings to her. All the best!"

"Thanks mum."

He felt his whole world crumble as he heard the phone's thud on the floor. It had slid from his hands which were shaking uncontrollably.

"What is it, Elibaby?" Naomi asked worried.

She had never seen him like this before. She put her arms around him as his tears fell.

She waited for him to be done crying before he said it, "Naomi, my mum has cancer."

"Oh no," Naomi couldn't believe this. She pulled him in closer for a hug, "I'm so sorry. Everything is going to be alright. She's going to beat this, ok?"

"I just can't believe she's held it back from me for so long. I feel guilty for feeling relieved when she wasn't checking up on me like she normally did. She was sick and I didn't know and I never bothered to check up on her."

"This isn't your fault ok. Everything is going to be alright."

She hugged him.

———————————

"So you are the Ashawo Dorcas girl who wants to steal our husbands from us," One woman spoke. With her were two other women who looked so angry that she was sure that they could actually spit fire from their eyes. She was just about to pass the East Wing after a hot night with Sir Daddy when they stopped her.

She wasn't sure whether to approach them or run. With the way they were looking angry, they could have been carrying acid or a gun. They approached her instead.

"What husbands?" She spoke. She didn't want her voice to come out frightened but it did.

"Ooh see this little girl o she wants to play dumb with us. I will slap the innocence out of your cosmetic face. You think we do not know what you have been doing with our men. You have no shame eh?" the other woman spoke up.

"You just came back from a hot steamy night with my husband right? I will skin you alive. Is that what your mother taught you? To be stealing people's husbands?" another said.

"Which kind of parents reared such a child?"

"I don't know mpo. Parents who breed such children are a danger and a menace to society."

"You if you don't want any trouble for yourself stay out of the businesses of our husbands. You hear?"

Dorcas shook. But only slightly. She had encountered worse. These women did not scare her.

"If only they stay out of mine. Your husbands come to me. I don't go to them," she countered and surprised all of them into silence. "I never understand why women fight over their boyfriends or husbands like that as if we beg them to come to us. Why do you come and fight the sidechick when he clearly left your matrimonial home and went to sleep somewhere else."

"But you knew they were married."

"And is it my job to stop it when they need me. It is not your job either. None of us are the problem. How sure are you that even if I stop seeing them they won't go on to find another? Men indeed are the weaker vessels," Dorcas said, suddenly feeling a little pity on them.

"Cheap girl."

"Slut."

"Bimbo."

"Ashawo ni."

"Dzulor!"

"Witch."

"You can call me all the names you want. I have been called worse by my own mother and father." She was exasperated and tired, "You know what? If you women had been doing your jobs very well, I wouldn't have been needed in the first place."

"You have the guts to say that to us?"

"Learn to respect little girl."

"I pray that you fall hopelessly in love, get married, have children and your husband cheats…so that you will know how it feels like."

"I am sorry to burst your bubble but I won't fall for any man and let my whole world revolve around him like you do. I don't have the time to feel insecure and for the record, I plan not to have children ever."

Her words only incensed them more as they took turns to slap her.

"Foolish girl, I hope our slaps teach you a lesson." And she watched with tearful eyes as they stomped away.

Dorcas bit her lips and willed the tears not to fall. She wasn't going to cry for the whole world to see. She hurried back to the room and opened the door with her key. When she was sure Sompa and Renee were asleep she let out all her pain into a pillow. She cried for her family and for herself. She thought about her father who had started her on this path and her own mother who had ignored it and had refused to report to the police.

She had always known that that man touched her. He would always tell her to come and sit on his lap and watch 'cartoons' with him. She would then feel him touching her and holding her breasts. One day he squeezed too hard and made her cry she run to tell her mother. Her mother had done nothing but beat her for being a bad child. There were bruises all over her body. She was just nine years old then. She still had the scars to show. He had continued until she ran away from the abuse and from poverty. Her mother was still giving birth even though they were poor. She hated her father. She hated her parents for being poor. She was tired of living a poor life. She wondered why poor people gave birth to more children when they knew they didn't have the means to take care of them.

She recalled the freedom she had felt when she had jumped onto the truck carrying cows to the city. It had been a lonely night having cows as company and smelling their dung. She remembered the hardships she had to go through just to save. When she realized she couldn't save enough in the city, she decided to use her body to get what she wanted. It worked like magic but she felt violated every time she did it until she became numb. She didn't feel anything at all. Perhaps she was meant to be bad. Perhaps this was her fate. She cried harder not caring that the makeup was all over her pillow.

CHAPTER TEN

Faith and fornication

"Oh my God, what a headache…." Araba murmured as she stirred on the bed and stared at the ceiling. It was Sunday again and she turned to see Maame with a glass of water and some pills.

"Goodmorning," she said with a bright smile. "Here's some medicine for your headache."

She sat up on the bed and reached out for them. "Thank you very much. My head feels so heavy as if I took a dozen sleeping pills."

She watched her as she took the pills and drank them down.

"Thanks." She handed over the glass to her.

"Do you remember what happened yesterday?"

"No, I know I went for the hall week jam but I

don't remember much after that." She laughed, "I must have been very drunk. I don't even remember how I came to even be on my own bed."

"Hmm…" Maame said and went quiet.

"Why what happened? Did Joey bring me to the room?"

Maame was quiet.

"Maame, what happened?" She was beginning to alarm her.

"Well, he brought you to the room alright but I think he wanted to sleep with you. I think he drugged you and made you unconscious. Although you were kissing him back, I'm not sure you knew what he was doing to you or what you were doing."

"What?!"

"Thank God, I came in just in time just when he was in the process of making you completely naked. And the annoying thing was that he was filming it all too."

"What?!" Araba was shocked, "I can't believe this guy." Why did he want to take advantage of her?

"He forgot to lock the door and when I came and saw what was going on, I was so livid."

"Oh my God, He must have taken so many pictures." She covered her face with her palms as she felt tears threatening to trickle down her cheeks.

"Don't worry I let him delete all of them before he left. I would have reported him yesterday but I needed to make sure that you were okay."

"Gosh! What if he had –" She began to whimper as she closed her legs tightly. She felt so violated.

"Well, he didn't and you've got to be careful around people like him. Most of the guys who are especially in final year I heard they prey on the first year students and make it look like they are in love with you. They just want to score a goal before they leave campus. They call it September or October Rush."

"If I get him eh …I wish I could report this." She said, "I'm really sorry for the way I treated you ever since you came to this room. Thanks for being there for me."

"You are welcome, dear and you will be fine," she encouraged as she gave her a warm hug, "Yeah, I was very hurt by your attitude and for the first time I thought God must have been wrong bringing me here. Now I know why He brought me into this room."

"Why?"

"It was for you."

And Araba smiled through her tears. She thought of how much she disliked God for making her sister leave. She was still not in talking terms with Him and wondered why He would think of her now.

"Oh so you couldn't go to church?"

"Yes."

"Really sorry about that."

"No it's fine. We have a special Sunday service this evening so I will be going. It's Testimony Evening, you really have to come I am sure you will enjoy it."

"I'll try…just remind me."

"Ok, I am going out to get some koko and

some koose, would you want some?"

"Yes of course, is it the one at Broad Way?"

"Yes."

"Then I am following you."

"Why?"

"I won't allow those boys to worry you."

"Don't worry, there was this lady who gave it to them at the gobɛ stand some time back, now I know how to fight them off so don't worry."

"Hahahaaa how was she?"

"She was phenomenal. I think she gave me a new lease of life and some courage too. Now I don't have to think of how many yards of wife material I am before I go there."

"Hahahaaa, you are crazy."

"Just sit back and relax ok."

"Alright, if you say so power puff girl."

"I've got to change."

She watched her as she changed her pyjamas and wore a top and a pair of jeans. But not until she caught sight of it.

"What's that?" Araba asked pointing.

"What?"

"That nasty scar on your right side."

"Oh you will find out soon enough."

"When?"

"When you come for Testimony evening at church."

Araba groaned, "You just want me to come. You are going to give a testimony?"

"Yeah and I want you to hear it."

"Now this I want to hear. What time is it?"

"6PM."

"Okay. I will come."

"Alright. I'm going. Wish me luck on those boys."

"Power puff girl, you will be fine."

"Thanks." She felt lighter as she stepped out. Now this was progress.

———————————————

She couldn't remember the last time she had attended church. Perhaps it was the day she had said a goodbye to her sister but her sister hadn't replied. Well, she couldn't remember. She felt like a stranger as she walked through the doors of the hall. She was late but she couldn't be bothered.

The place was so packed and she was grateful when an usher led her to an empty seat at the front.

"You are all welcome once again to today's Testimony service and as most of you know, we have testimony service every first Sunday of a new month and it is always a great honour to attend this service and listen to all the miracles and experiences that God has shared with His people. We have quite a number of people going to share their testimonies tonight and it is my hope and prayer that as you listen to them, God will make those miracles happen in your life."

"Amen."

"You are also going to encounter him like never before."

"Amen."

"Thank you very much, now we can start. Can we have the first person?" A tall fair girl approached the pulpit amidst applause.

"Hi my name is Afua, and I am a member of the choir."

"Hello Afua."

"God has been indeed good. A couple of months before if you had told me that God has been good, I will reply without really believing it. I needed money. My school fees hadn't been paid in full, my mother was sick and all the bills were piling up. All the money was used to pay my mother's hospital bills for three whole months, I didn't know what to do or what to eat. I was desperate but I thank God for my roommate who helped me throughout those trying times when I finally told her that I was struggling. She gave me food to eat and money to take care of myself. I am really grateful. Just last week, I got a scholarship to continue my education with and wow! I just couldn't believe it."

"Wow, Hallelujah!" some members of the congregation got up and clapped.

"Now all my tuition and accommodation is being covered. I called my mother today and she's feeling better. The doctor said that although she might not be able to walk again, she'll live. I just want to say that God is able to do exceedingly abundantly above all that you can ever ask or imagine. So thank you Jesus for making me smile after the storm."

"Wow we tap into that favour," someone screamed.

People clapped and clapped and clapped. Maame walked onto the stage and waited for the clapping to reside and began to speak.

"Hi everyone, my name is Maame and I'm a member of Bible Bookish."

"Hi Maame."

"My testimony is about how God saved me from cancer. You might not believe this but I am standing here without a big intestine but I am feeling whole. I have had five surgeries. One Caesarean and four major surgeries."

The auditorium went quiet as they listened.

"Last two years, I had cancer of the colon. Anytime I went to the hospital they had to cut a part of the colon where the cancer appeared and each time they did that the length of my intestines decreased until they had cut away a huge chunk of it. After the last operation they declared me hopeless. This was after I had completed SHS. I was supposed to have come to the university earlier but for the disease. I had become like a vegetable. The doctors gave me just six months to live and they sent me home to die."

Araba listened with pain as she wondered the pain her friend must have gone through and she thought of her big sister, Esaaba.

"Death was something I was scared of. It wasn't the fact that I wasn't going to be here anymore or that I will be stuck in a world where I couldn't feel a thing. What scared me was the fact that I wouldn't get to experience all that I wanted to experience. University, love, marriage, motherhood and the sheer satisfaction of seeing my purpose become a reality. My parents were scared for me too. They spoke to the doctors who recommended a Total Colectomy which is a surgical procedure to remove all of the colon," she continued, "They seal your anus and they bypass the anus and go through the side of the tummy. With this process, body waste comes out through the tube from the side of the tummy with the attachment of a colectomy bag. I imagined it was embarrassing and painful to wake up each day having to see your poop collected in a bag. Hahahaa guys I never thought I would be faced with the chance to be grateful that I could poo normally. So be grateful."

Tears began to trickle down as Araba listened.

"Sometimes when I look back, I cry because that experience was very painful and I wouldn't want to wish it on anybody. I decided not to have the total colestomy done even though the doctors told me that it was risky because there was a high chance the cancer could appear again and this time it could attack my small intestine. But I had to take that risk and trust God. The doctors had to resort to a lot of cutting and joining to make me feel better. I left the hospital with a part of me in a surgical bowl. I knew that I had taken a big risk and I did care. The fear of six whole months to live began to paralyse me and my parents and the church never ceased to pray for me. They kept on saying, 'Have faith, have faith.' And I did. In that state you have to keep hope alive and prepare to die; what else can you do?

"I quite remember one morning waking up in those six months and opening my Bible to read. It had been long since I had talked to God. What I was going through was enough to separate me from the love of God, or so I thought. I didn't understand why he had to bring such a disease my way and I hated him for it. If he was indeed the God of love, why didn't he stop it from the beginning? Why did this cancer eat away at my body? I didn't understand but that morning, I picked up my Bible and I read the story of Shadrach, Meshach and Abednego. Most of you are quite familiar with the story.

"Before they were thrown into the furnace they said, 'If we are thrown into the blazing furnace, the God we serve is able to deliver us from your hand. But even if he does not we want you to know that we will not serve your gods or worship the image you have set up.' The thing is God allows certain bad stuff to happen in our lives. Sometimes it might not be a disease, it might be the death of a loved one or the loss of a job or a shut door but he implores us to have faith in His perfect will. Reading that scripture again brought so much peace. I knew that even if God didn't heal me and I had to die then I must accept my fate. If we knew all his plans then he wouldn't be God.

"Six months after and almost two years I am still here even in the face of what the doctors told me and in the face of what Science logically said. I don't know why my life was spared perhaps I was supposed to meet you someday at this very moment to tell you that God is still in the miracle business and even if you seem not to be getting healed or not to be getting that job you so wish or it seems every open door closes to you, just rest in this. He knows the end from the beginning. Just keep on having faith and keep on worshipping Him. He knows and he is here." She ended with a smile, "Thank you."

Araba smiled back through her tears. She didn't care that she was in a church filled with people and that they would see her tears. She still remembered when they had received the news one Sunday. Esaaba had been in final year, in her second semester preparing to complete her degree. Esaaba was just returning from church and was in a trotro. The trotro collided with a big truck. The impact threw her out of the window and onto the road and instead of stopping, the truck sped and run over her body. Everyone thought she was dead when they rushed her to the hospital. She was in a coma for several days. They had prayed. The church had prayed and fasted. They had brought bottles of communion for her to drink, they had anointed her whole body from her head to her feet with anointing oil. Everyone had encouraged them to have faith and they had until a week later she died.

She was just returning from church; what happened to all the prayers of protection her sister had prayed that morning. Why had she been the only one who died in that accident? Where was God? Her sister was the sweetest and had served Him all her life, why did she have to be taken away so early and so painfully? Her mother had lost the spark from her eyes, she never attended church with her husband anymore; she just sat at home staring into the ceiling and her father seemed to be lost and confused in his own grief. She wondered how he got to stand infront of the congregation every Tuesday, Wednesday, Saturday and Sunday. Araba couldn't remember the last time she had heard her parents laugh. She was angry at God. She and God were no longer friends.

She had burned her Bible a long time ago.

"Wow that was an amazing testimony, God is indeed still in the miracle business. I want to thank you all for making yourself available to share the good things God has done in your life. My prayer is that God keep blessing you and keeping us in good health. If you are here and you want to give your life to Christ or you have given your life to Christ but you have backslidden and you feel that you can never come back to Him again, please come forward."

Araba stood up and walked forward.

She felt peace.

"Mr. Asaase, please leave else you will cause a scene…"

"You this Gabon girl, you think you are so smart to allow me to buy you a phone and then you go scot free?"

The old man was back again and this time he had caught Renee right behind the door.

"I am sorry-"

"You are sorry now, aren't you? After I called you so many times. I bought you a phone and you thought it was free bonto," he continued in anger, "You have two options. You either give me back the phone I bought you or do what I ask you to."

"I never asked you to get me a phone. You insisted."

"Well… if you don't do what I ask then I want it back."

"Renee just give him back the phone."

"Stay out of my business, Sompa."

"Ah but you think he giving you the latest iPhone is for free?" Dorcas said slyly, "You've got to work for it baby."

"Give me the phone!" He threatened, "I have

my boys near and we would not hesitate to beat you up."

At that Renee slightly shook as she hurriedly removed her chip and handed the phone back to him.

"Better!" He said suddenly looking at Dorcas. "I think you are fit to handle this treasure, my Queen."

"Awww I am flattered. Thank you, Sir for this kind gesture but I have my hands already full."

"Oh that's too bad. Can I have your number to know when you are less busy?"

"I guess that would be okay." She giggled as she rattled off the numbers to him. If she saw the incredulous looking mask on Renee's face then she didn't acknowledge it.

"Thank you so much, I will be giving you a call soon." He drawled out, "What's your lovely name?"

"Dorcas."

"Beautiful Gazelle," He uttered, "I will talk to you soon."

As soon as he left, Dorcas sneered at Renee,

"But you paa, if you really want to get into this kind of game, come to me so that I teach you well."

"Yeah right, we already know what you've been doing," Renee remarked and muttered, "Ashawo."

CHAPTER ELEVEN

Sour grapes

Stephanie stared at the printed results. No these figures looked so wrong. Stephanie remembered clearly that this girl had managed to get the lowest marks in the class after the exams. *That Dorcas girl, how come she got all 'As' in her work?* This was really fishy. There were rumours she had heard about a girl sleeping with some of the lecturers for marks. She didn't want to think it was Dorcas but if it was her…hmmm. She knew that the lecturer she worked for, Professor Bediako already had rumours surrounding him. She had heard of his escapades in his office and anytime she looked at his table she wondered how many girls he had touched.

The annoying thing about the whole charade

was that the serious students were the ones going to suffer. She wasn't going to allow that. She was going to put a stop to this. She decided to call Dorcas to find out.

"Timothy, please tell Dorcas to come and see me ASAP," she told one student.

"Okay."

After about fifteen minutes later, Dorcas came in in her usual short clothes, giving a performance as she walked.

"Yes TA, what can I do for you?" she said with a smirk that wonderfully matched her bright pink lips.

"I don't understand something. I recall you got low marks for your exams and I can't believe what I am seeing here." She asked, "How come you were the fifth highest in the class?"

She smiled sweetly, "Really? Perhaps it is the doing of the Lord. Those all nights spent at Fawohodie Park were truly not in vain."

She hated the way the young lady lied through her teeth and didn't crack. It looked like lying was second nature to her.

"Well, I'm going to see to it that it is truly not in vain." Stephanie said, "You can go now."

"Ok." Dorcas walked away but made a mental note to talk to Professor Bediako. She walked to his door.

"Hello, Professor Bediako."

"Yes please come in."

"Your TA has noticed something in my marks and I don't appreciate that."

"Really? Don't worry Dorcas, I will talk to her."

"You better," and she sauntered away.

Stephanie came in shortly after.

"Hello Sir."

"Hello Stephanie. What can I do for you?"

"Please Sir, I need to talk to you about something. I see something wrong with one particular girl's marks. I recall very clearly that she had one of the lowest marks but I'm seeing all 'As' here. Why?"

"Well, she deserved it," he didn't think he needed to answer to her.

"But…."

"Yes I realized her answers didn't follow the marking scheme but when I read carefully, she seems to have got some real sense."

"Uhmm ok."

"So don't worry, Dorcas is doing fairly well. She's making a lot of progress."

"Ok, I guess that's good news right?"

"Right," He said deliberately looking into her eyes with annoyance. "Stephanie, don't be too hard on her okay. She really is trying."

"Yes Sir." *Yeah she is really trying to warm your bed,* she thought, "I'll be on my way."

And he nodded.

However, Stephanie wasn't really convinced as she noticed Dorcas going in and out of his office so many times. There was something definitely going on and she needed to tell someone. Fortunately, she didn't have to go and look for someone to tell. That person came to her.

"Hello dear lady, how are you doing?"

"I'm doing fine, Madam and you?" She welcomed her with a bright smile.

"I'm also doing well."

"Umm Madam, your husband is still in a meeting but I can call him for you –" Stephanie offered, standing up.

"That won't be necessary. I came to see you."

"Wow, to what honour do I owe this visit?"

"Can I see you outside for a minute?" She whispered, looking around.

"Yes."

As soon as they were outside, the woman looked comfortable.

"What is it, Madam?"

"I've heard rumours that my husband has been cheating on me with some of the students but I do not know whether it's true. So I decided to come and ask, have you noticed any unusual activity going on with my husband and his students? Please I need to know what he has been up to. I need to. If you were in my position, you would want to."

"Um, Madam, I haven't seen the deed with my eyes but I have seen a particular student going to his office sometimes and it looks like she gets all 'As' too."

"Wow, this truly explains his constant bookings to the Sunny Side Hotel on Sundays."

"I'm sorry I had to tell you this, Madam."

"No, no, it's okay, I just needed to confirm my suspicions," she said, "I need to go home now. Thank you very much."

"You are welcome."

"James, what have I done to deserve this treatment from you?" the woman cried out, "Why do you keep doing this? Why do you cause me so much embarrassment?" She slapped him so many times and pulled his shirt, as tears flowed down her cheeks.

So she knew. Why were women always the first to know when something was up? Her frustration seemed to heighten by the minute but he didn't care. He looked at the tearful eyes of the woman he had spent twenty years of his life with and realised how much pain she must have been going through. He wondered how his two children would take yet another case of his infidelity. But he didn't care. She didn't satisfy him sexually and a man has needs.

He turned his back to her.

"So now, I am talking and you are turning your back to me?" she snapped, throwing a pillow hard at his head.

"Tell me Ama, tell me, what do you expect when you don't satisfy me?"

"Wow, so this is what this has always been about? I have told you the reason, why can't you just be patient with me?" she called out in frustration, "What about the vows we said to each other at the altar; for better for worse? What happened to the love, James?"

"You and I both know that those words were just a formality."

"I can't endure such pain, embarrassment and disrespect anymore. I'm not going to fight for this marriage seeing that you aren't even sorry that you have been caught out of your lies. We will definitely see in this house what will become of you. You will see where power lies."

Ama Bediako turned her back to him and slammed the door for good measure when she walked out of the room. How many times hadn't she gone down on her knees to pray for her husband's cheating ways? How many times hadn't she gone for counselling at the church; they always seemed to think that she was the one doing something wrong. The church counsellor once prescribed watching the War Room. She was done. She was done warring with the enemy for her husband. Perhaps her husband was the enemy. She was done tolerating the disrespect and the shame. With all the rumours going around, she was sure that even her students did not respect her anymore. 'This man will surely get what is coming to him,' she muttered as she vainly tried to stop the tears.

CHAPTER TWELVE

Unwarranted permissions

"Ah why do these Mallams keep sending me requests on Facebook?" Naomi asked, looking at her phone. "Look at this one o…he cannot even spell correctly yet he's selling medicine for cleverness."

"Eii these Mallams will not kill us o! The world has indeed become a global village. Hahaha Mallams are joining the social media rage. When you delete one Mallam, it is like a thousand more follow," Sompa quipped.

"He's called Mallam Yaazo! This is too funny… let me read it to you." Naomi called out, "If you born poor is not your mistake but if you die poor it's your mistake. You was not born to suffer, like what people say, all fingers are not equal but why must you been the shortest finger. Never judge a book according to its cover. You may think that a sleeping snake is dead, the only thing you can do is to touch its tail. I am the great Mallam. The Worshipper of the seventh sea. Mallam is here to help those who are lacking this kind of problems, luck of financial problems, lotto number, visa, high spirit, clearver, lucky, protection, all types of sickness, blood money, married problem, you want position in a workplace, someone is owning you; I can work and the person will send it back. Can't talk much, call me."

"Eiii Hahaahaaa, See this Mallam too, he better use his own medicine on himself, he needs it."

"You block them 120 times and they come back with 400 more. It's funny how they look so desperate on social media. Like if you want money, can't you conjure it up for yourself rather than call for people to seek your services?"

"Perhaps they cannot use their juju for themselves."

"That's some weird spiritual policy. I'm deleting him kraa, all of them."

Sompa suddenly giggled as she stared at her phone.

"Eii, what or who is making my sister laugh?" Nao asked wondering why she had a bright smile on her face, "Is it that guy again? The guy who's name sounds like an adverb."

Sompa laughed, "Eii Nao, always good with descriptions. Yes that's Percy."

"And I get that you are falling in love with him."

"Oh no, we are just friends."

"Tell me, Sompa which friend will come and play his guitar at your closed birthday party and serenade you with music? Keep telling that to yourself but don't tell that to me. I know how your face lights up when you receive a message from him."

"Oh Nao la."

"Ayoo, the way you people have been meeting dierr, I am just watching you o."

"I'm also watching the Nao-Eli love which

seems to be going strong paa."

"Oh gyae me."

"It's been awhile I heard from him, where is he?"

"He's gone to visit his mother. She is sick and has breast cancer."

"Gosh, I hope she gets better."

"I hope so too. She's a really wonderful woman. She is always calling to check up on me."

"Some mother-in-law things…just tell me when the wedding is and the wedding colours and I will be there."

"Crazzzy girl. I'm going to see Nolan and later remove these braids from my hair, ok? I have got to check up on how final year is treating him."

"I know right. You haven't been a good sister."

"I will see you later, Sompa."

"Ok."

Sompa went back to her texting with Percy and smiled again at one of his many jokes. It had been so many weeks and she missed him. The night of the kiss had left her angry and bothered but she couldn't help but think how wonderful it had been. After she had left, he apologized and said he was sorry. This felt different and she was already brimming with new feelings for Percy. It was true what they said, once you did it, you would want to do it again and again.

Sompa already felt guilty when she went to the church one Wednesday. Even though it had been just a kiss, it still felt big and wrong to her. After Pastor Benjamin had preached on How to have a Godly relationship, people were given the opportunity to ask questions. One question that got her attention was, 'is kissing wrong in a Christian relationship?"

And the preacher said, "It is very wrong. Kissing is working on the door upstairs for permission to work on the door downstairs. The thing is why do you start the thing when you very well know that it can lead to sex? The Bible said, 'Do not arouse or awaken love until it so desires.' We modern Christians think that now kissing and all the other stuff is okay once it is not sex but I tell you, it is still fornication."

But what happens when you already have?

Sompa thought as someone in the church shouted, "Etwiii Obi o." And everyone laughed. Sompa found herself always going over to his place and indulging in what she wasn't supposed to indulge in. Percy was so smooth and overwhelming. He was such a dream and he loved her.

P: *I guess meeting you is the reason I came to church*

S: *Perhaps*

P: *I know it sounds corny or cheesy*

S: *It is corny and cheesy and it sounds foody. But I get you.*

P: *Hahahaaaa*

9pm

P: *Asleep?*

S: *No dear*

P: *Thinking about you*

S: *Me too. Going to bed soon?*

P: *Naa. Not feeling sleepy yet*

S: *Oohk thought your lights were on now*

P: *Nopes. Darkness Galore. Dumsor is back. Just lying down now*

S: *Oh Sorry President Jake has done it again o*

P: Heheheeee welcome to the world of Ghanaian Politics

S: I thought after they released the 'Jake aba' bread things will change o

P: They are all the same. There is no change in value, the value is the same.

S: ikr! Look at what that song did to the one pesewa coin. Heheheeee, Ghana my beloved country.

P: Enough about our country. Really miss you babe and I think I want you. It's bad

S: Miss you so much too. Very much. Really much. What are we going to do?

P: Wanna come over?

S: Yes sure

Those were the only words that moved her and that night they went very far. They had sex and Sompa could not believe what they had both done. That night, she cried as she covered her breasts.

"I can't believe we did this! I just can't. I'm leaving this place and I am not coming back ever again."

"Why are you making it sound like you are the

innocent one; like you didn't know what you were doing? I'm sick of your holier than thou attitude," Percy spat out.

"Wow Percy, just wow. And I thought you were a gentleman." She was shocked and at the same time filled with regret. She should have never set eyes on him. She should have heeded to the advice of the preacher.

As soon as she left the room, Percy removed the hidden device from behind the curtains. Now he had the evidence. All he needed to do was to show the boys and to break up whatever he had with her.

CHAPTER THIRTEEN

Letting go

"Hey Sompa," Percy said the next two days after the incident happened.

"Yes Percy? Glad to hear from you after two whole days of silence," she said sarcastically with annoyance as she stared at the opened books on the bed. "What do you want?"

"I called to let you know that we should break up."

There was a long pause as Sompa took it in. What did she expect? That he will come back and console her or they would still be together? He really just wanted to sleep with her after all but it still hurt.

"Right…" she said in the bravest voice that she could muster but her throat was already threatening to sound like she was crying.

"This is so hard, Sompa…It's better if I be the guy who broke up with you because of the issue of lust than be the guy who made you have sex before marriage."

What was this guy even saying? He was already that guy, Sompa silently argued with herself. "Alright Percy."

"We need to let go and let God."

"Uhuh yup."

"I have to be holy and you have to be too. We are children of God."

"Ok."

"Paul says in Romans that our reasonable sacrifice to God is to present our bodies as living sacrifices…Holy and acceptable to God. Our bodies are a presentation and a sacrifice."

"Are you seriously quoting Scriptures to me now, Percy?"

"I'm sorry Sompa, we need Jesus more than we need each other. I need Him to fix me up. You need Him too…to restore you to your path. God has called us for far greater things than messing around and going back to ask for forgiveness. We need to stop seeing each other and get serious with God. I believe you know that God wants to use you? You can't be used by God and someone else."

"Really, Percy? Thank you for letting me know that you were just using me."

"I'm sorry Sompa, I don't want to be likened to the dog who goes back to its own vomit."

"I've heard you loud and clear, Preacher Percy. If you had been preaching and pious from the start, we wouldn't have gotten here. Bye."

Sompa cried into her pillow when she hang up. Her mind recalled the goals she had written in her diary. None of them had worked, none of them. She covered her whole body with a cloth and wallowed in her own pain and heartbreak. She heard her phone ring but ignored it. She didn't want to talk to anybody.

It was a loud evening at the Adinkra Common

room where the guys often played pool and chess and watched football on the big screen.

Manchester United and Liverpool had played and they had just ended the football argument and had moved on to a more interesting topic: Girls!

"Charley…there's this fine chick I've been meaning to catch Charley but she dey do me roff," Joey said in mock pain.

"You be jon boy, last year's October Rush wasn't good for you and this year being your final year you want try force and score nil? Ebeii!" Larry joked.

"Hahahaa he dey fear. That's why he for support Liverpool la," one guy called Teabag said.

"AAAAAH, that be why!" Damboro let out his hilarious laughter.

"Hahahaa I now know sey your sickness and diagnosis ebe Gynophobia."

"Shut up for der I go fi tell your girlfriend the other side meals you dey have."

"Jealousy go kill you oh, land one just one and let us hail you."

"Hahahaa baako suroo! One is scaryyy."

"But guys you for wise up o…no be book you go chop at dawn."

"So who got the jackpot this week?" Larry asked, downing a tot of beer.

"I did o…this week I finally landed her la," Percy spoke up.

"Ebe the same chick you dey find for church?"

"Yes."

"The one who you dey play tunes for on Sophia, your guitar?"

"The very same one la."

"I thought you feel am o. Se you play some love song bi on her birthday."

"I was playing a stringed instrument but there were no strings attached," Percy said, a little annoyed that the guys did not believe him.

"I no fit believe you. She be Chrife too much."

"Eheeh, even the devil cannot tempt am how much more you mere man?"

"It's true la, I was able to break down the walls of Jericho and get into the promised land but mehn it wasn't easy."

"I won't believe it till I see some evidence…that girl I for respect am too much. She be Christian, she dey sing lovely and she get head too."

"Well, you want evidence? I'll show you evidence."

He removed his phone from his pocket and passed it round for the guys to see the pictures.

"Oh charley yawa pae o, the girl be fiiiiiine too."

"Ohh this one dierr your pics and videos be tight o."

"Ah but you paa, why you for record am?" Randy suddenly asked.

"So that I can give you evidence."

"You be dangerous boy paa. You no dey force. Ebe your sister or your mother like you go share?"

"Oh shun the talk for der, Randy, these videos and pics be lit. Bombs ne mines," Larry commented.

"She is such a lovely vixen and chick," Joey remarked.

"You enjoyed o…welcome to the table of

men," Larry declared, extending his hand for a shake.

"Seriously? Really?" Randy asked as he got up incensed, "If this is the table of men then I'm out. I can't believe that I am even hanging out with you guys. Percy, even if you did it why do you have to disrespect the girl's image and take pics and videos? Huh?"

"Tweaaa! Why are you talking as if you are a perfect guy? As if we don't know all your escapades," Percy fumed.

"I know you know them but at least I don't go around documenting them. You are such a twerp."

Percy got up, his full height short compared to Randy's. "Call me a twerp again…" He demanded, clenching his fists. He had forgotten all about the phone as he raged inside against Randy.

"Chcap twcrp. Coward."

Percy landed a punch on Randy's chest and Randy returned the punch, hitting Percy in his groin. The other guys tried unsuccessfully to separate the two boys as they kicked each other and scuffled and by the time they were done, Percy had a swollen eye and his shirt was losing some buttons and had become crumbled and dirty.

"You don't do that to a girl ever," Randy said in a dangerous tone as he pointed at him.

"Look at the pot calling the kettle black."

"Unlike you I don't destroy their image. You will definitely get what is coming to you." He looked around at them menacingly and walked out.

CHAPTER FOURTEEN

Shot, framed and hanged

"Hello Ladies, I am Caleb….I am here to introduce you to a business opportunity that will change your life." Caleb stood in the doorway of room 64 as he stared at the two ladies in the room. He hoped that all the walking to the eighth floor will pay off after these girls buy into his idea.

"Um…okay?" Araba said. She had just returned from morning lectures and needed some sleep break before the afternoon lecture starts.

"What are your names?"

"I'm Araba."

"And I'm Maame."

"Oohk nice to meet you. Do you have 700 Ghana cedis?"

"No I don't."

"Okay, do you have 1000?"

"Ah are you from Posterity Life International?" Maame asked.

"Yes…how do you know?"

"Because you guys are more than Jehovah's Witnesses."

"We are not interested oh."

"Oh you won't even let me tell you more about our products and services."

"I know them all dear. Thanks for passing through."

"Oh Maame, you *yawaad* the boy o."

"These people like to preach about money too much. I don't trust them especially where they do not sell the actual product to you but try to recruit you with your money as foundation."

"Heeeheee eii Maame. Didn't know you were wild too."

"Hahaaha everyone has a wild side."

"I like your wild side, heheheeee."

Araba heard a notification on her phone and she picked it up.

"Gosh!" Araba covered her mouth as she

stared at the contents on her phone.

"Why? What has happened?"

"Look! Nsoroma University student sex video released."

They both watched the video and noticed that the video was too clear for comfort. Whoever was with her had managed to position the camera at an angle that completely hid the guy's face.

"Ooh my, this face looks really familiar…"

"I'm so sad for her."

"Who could do this dastardly thing to her?"

"This could have happened to me, Maame with that Joey guy," Araba said, tears almost trickling down her face, "I can imagine how she must be feeling right now."

"God please comfort her."

"Asem o. God punish the boy who did this."

———————————

"She looks like the girl in the sex tape."

"She really does look like her."

"Isn't she a chorister at that church that meets

at the Dome Hall?"

"Look at her, Ashawo."

She started feeling uneasy as soon as lectures closed. She was getting too many disapproving stares as if they wanted to kill her. What was going on? She tried to turn on her data but it seemed she was out of credit. At that moment she got a call from Naomi.

"Sompa, what is going on?" It was Naomi and she sounded worried. Really worried.

"What do you mean by what is going on? I'm the confused one here…"

"You know what I'll see you when you get to the room ok?"

"Ok?" Sompa wondered why her world seemed to spiral around her. Why were people staring at her? And why was Dorcas standing at the car park, waving her over.

"Hey what's up?"

"I want to give you a ride today and I'm not taking no for an answer."

"Why? I can walk on my own."

"Trust me, you wouldn't want to."

She opened the car door for her and watched as she got in and strapped herself in.

"Now tell me what is really going on?" Sompa turned to ask.

"Why? You do not know what is going on? Where is your phone?"

"It's here but my data is off."

"Hmm, that's why."

"Why what's wrong?"

"Let's get you to the room first." Now she was in suspense. If even Dorcas couldn't tell her whatever it was then there was trouble.

She drove really fast and helped her out of the car and walked with her to the room. A group of guys snickered when they saw Sompa.

"What are you staring at?" Dorcas snapped at them as she held onto Sompa's hand tightly.

"Your friend is a slut and that also makes you one."

"You better shut your mouth." She reassured, "Don't mind them, Sompa."

But Sompa didn't say anything, she was just confused and scared out of her mind.

"Dorcas, why is everyone calling me an Ashawo, why?" she asked once they were safe and away from the prying eyes.

"There was a leaked sex tape today – just this afternoon and you looked just like the person in it."

"Let me see."

"No, it will be too much to watch for you."

"Let me see, Dorcas."

Dorcas took out her phone and started the video. She watched Sompa tentatively as a mix of emotions passed across her face.

"Oh no! So that Percy guy recorded it?!" Sompa watched as tears cascaded down her cheeks. The phone in her hands shook and Dorcas hurriedly took it away.

"Dor--- Dorcas … what do I do now?" she said in between sniffles.

"You take it all in and rest, everything is going to be fine."

"Dorcas, I'm all over social media! How can everything be fine?" She cried. What will her family and church say if they saw this? The embarrassment. The shame. The disappointment of it all. How was everything going to be alright? She wished the world would swallow her up. She curled herself into a ball on her bed and covered herself to hide her tears.

"I'm going to get some supplies, Sompa trust me you will be fine."

She mumbled a reply as she watched Dorcas go. Her phone rang and she picked it up hurriedly.

"So you couldn't just let me be after using me and breaking up with me? You just had to record everything and post it on social media?" She lashed out.

"Sompa, please listen," Percy was in anguish, "Trust me I didn't release those pictures. Yes I recorded everything but I didn't mean for them to come out like this."

"Oh so you recorded without my consent? I regret the day I met you."

"Please Sompa, I'm sorry…it's one of the boys –" She hung up on him. The young troubled lady recalled with regret those days of her first year in the University. In the video, she couldn't even recognize herself anymore. *What have I become?* She asked herself? Where was the lady who shunned unhealthy love relationships? Where was the lady who once preached purity? Where was she? How did she get here?

Looking back, she didn't even know who to blame; her desire to try out something new; her curiosity or the influence of her roommates who had boyfriends visiting them and who talked about guys endlessly. Percy had made sure his face had not been shown in the video. She switched off her phone and covered her face with a pillow. She could see people judging her in the dark pools of their eyes.

"Sompa, are you okay?" Naomi and Nolan rushed into the room wearing worried looks.

"I saw your face in those pictures and in the video, why didn't you tell me he was such a prick to record you. How could you, Sompa?" She pulled away the covers over Sompa and watched as she sat up. Naomi couldn't help but hug her friend.

"Please Nao, I didn't know he was recording

anything. I don't need this right now. I already feel like nothing, I don't need you to come and add to my worthlessness."

She was filled with guilt and remorse. She had adopted so many faces now and so many colours just to fit in, she didn't know what her true colours were anymore and she wanted to just end it all.

"Where is the boy who did this to you?" Nolan asked, dangerously calm.

"His name is Percy, he is a fifth year medical student and he stays at the Groomies Hostel near the hospital," Naomi replied.

"I'm going to beat the life out of him," Nolan fumed. He was really angry; who would do this to the girl who was like a sister to him and who he liked secretly? He left the room with clenched fists and Naomi knew that she didn't want to stop whatever he did to that guy. He deserved it.

"So what are you going to do now?" She sat by her friend as she held her hands.

"I don't know what to do, can you leave me alone?" Sompa snapped. All she wanted was to be left alone. Why didn't people get that?

"Ok, if you say so. But if you need my help, I'm just a room away, ok?" she said reluctantly as she turned to leave and Sompa didn't bother giving her an answer.

She could say that she couldn't believe what Percy was capable of; but she could. He swept her off her feet the first time she met him. She said yes because he was a Christian, loved gospel songs, was studying to become a doctor and had great dreams and ambitions and oh, he could even play the guitar! He was such a beautiful nightmare that had walked into her life. She should have known when he started performing 'Cardiopulmonary resuscitation' on her.

The first time, she was too shocked to react and she had fled the room, running through the evening rain that poured like God's tears. But the next time and the next, she gradually gave in, numbing her conscience in the process. She was also to blame.

Sompa cried uncontrollably into a pillow as she wondered how she was going to live with it. Everyone who knew her had seen the videos and the pictures and everyone judged her. The next few days were spent in bed as she didn't think it will be okay to come out just yet. Elise her classmate and friend brought her a letter from the Dean of Students.

She went through so many processes at the Dean of Students office and stood before a disciplinary committee who asked her of the guy's name. After everything, she could barely stand and Nolan and Naomi had to help her out through it all.

She couldn't even bear to face her parents now. Her parents! And her siblings! She slumped; this was just too much. She stood up all of a sudden as the only way to end it all came to her. She felt so empty so she emptied the little bag of angry looking pills.

She took the rope and stared at the ceiling fan. She climbed onto the bunkbed at the top and carefully tied the rope around the fan.

She swallowed and cleaned away her tears. She needed to be strong for this. She needed to end her life. With shaking hands and her nightie covered with tears, she edged closer to the rope. This was it. She wasn't going to leave any note for anyone. She didn't deserve what she had done to them and so she was going to do them the honour of taking the exit of this world first.

She shook as she put the other end of the rope around her neck. She was just about to swing from the bed to allow the piece of rope to tighten around her neck and finally choke her to death when her roommate, Renee came in through the door. Renee stood wide-eyed with shock written all over her face.

"Don't," she said, coming towards her, "Please don't. No matter what you have done or what you are going through, don't go this way."

Renee quickly but carefully came towards her roomie and took off the rope. She cradled Sompa as the lady cried on her shoulders. She saw the bag of pills and figured Sompa must have emptied its contents down her throat. She needed to act fast.

"Sompa, you are still needed. Don't end your life like this. I can imagine what you are going through and I don't need to tell you that your actions have led to this. We all make mistakes, dear. But committing suicide makes you a coward; it takes strength to rise above and face the consequences. We are all here to help you. Please don't give in to death."

"You don't understand, Renee, I have failed God, I have failed my family terribly; I have failed this life," she cried, "I don't think I can live with the shame. I hate myself so much!"

"Don't worry my friend, I am here for you and don't mind those who pass judgement. We are all fallible; some fornicate and their sins don't come out in the open. Just because yours has come out doesn't make what they also do in secret any less, what happens is your reaction toward it." Sompa whimpered. Renee hurriedly asked for help from some guys outside who quickly rushed her to the hospital. Naomi and Elikem followed to the hospital when they heard it.

"It's my fault…I should have seen the signs and warned her. I shouldn't have left her when she wanted to be alone."

"Don't blame yourself, let's just make sure

she's ok."

Two hours later, it was the respirator that woke her up and she was glad when she saw her friends by her side. Naomi, Dorcas, Nolan, Elikem and Reinee. Her family too were by her side and they smiled when she opened her eyes.

"God I thank you," she heard her mother let out a sigh of relief as she rubbed her palms.

"We are all here for you, Sompa, you are needed," her father calmly said as he kissed her forehead.

"Thanks Dad, thank you everyone."

"You will be fine, Sompa just one day at a time," Elikem encouraged.

"I will," she smiled weakly, "Hope your mother is doing better?"

"Yes, she is. The chemotherapy went well but even though she may lose one of her breasts she will be fine."

And she nodded and gave him a winsome smile.

Though she had people around her who still loved her, people didn't let her forget. But it was the love from her family that kept her going. Percy was eventually expelled and charged and Sompa had to begin picking up the pieces.

CHAPTER FIFTEEN

True colours

"Professor Bediako, I don't appreciate the fact that I'm trailing with French fried fishes in my midsemester examinations. I thought they were As?" Dorcas was in his office angry and she hated that the professor had breached the contract they had had. The results had just been released and almost everyone had seen their marks.

The old man looked up from the laptop he was working on and raked his eyes over her. He knew she would come…he had been expecting her. Anytime a Shatta song played on the radio, he couldn't help but think of her. She was really overwhelmingly gorgeous when she was angry. He noticed the beads of sweat that came down from the edges of her purple wig and almost reached out to wipe them away but with the look she wore, he restrained himself.

"Well, that's because the academic auditors came around and I do not want any trouble," he drawled out.

"You don't want any trouble so where does this put me?" She continued in a dangerous tone, "I have fulfilled my end of the bargain and I expect you to fulfill yours."

"Well…changing them back is going to be difficult."

"I don't care if it's going to be or not. I don't care how you are going to do it. All I care about is seeing those As smiling at me on my academic reports."

"I'm sorry Dorcas, but I can't put my reputation on the line."

"Oh so is that how this is going to be? You didn't ask about my reputation when you demanded that I sleep with you, knowing how desperate I was?"

"I'm sorry, I just cannot do it. If anyone, especially the auditors found out that I changed your marks I will not have the opportunity to be a lecturer again."

"Well then start saying your goodbyes to being a lecturer. You may have slept with so many girls and gotten away with it but this time you messed with the wrong girl."

"Dorcas, what do you mean?" He asked, suddenly worried. The pit in his stomach widened.

"Oh you shall find out soon enough," she said menacingly as she turned around and walked away.

Dorcas was so pissed but glad that she had kept all the Whatsapp messages they had had and pictures. It was therefore no surprise when she got into her car and drove to the Dean of Students Office to report the case. The D.O.S., Professor Crabbe was appalled and surprised by the evidence and forwarded it all to the Vicc Chancellor. In a matter of weeks, a disciplinary committee and the University Council was set up to investigate the matter.

Professor Bediako's TA, Stephanie was

summoned to answer some questions truthfully and his wife as well. He was later called and in the room he became agitated when the evidence was presented before him.

So this is what Dorcas had been referring to. He knew she was a smart girl but not that smart. *I am in trouble*, he thought as he felt sweat trickling down his face. The air conditioned room suddenly became hot as he stared into the grim and stern faces of the authorities. People he once called friends and colleagues did not have smiles for him and they condemned and judged him with their eyes.

"Professor Bediako, it has come to our attention that you have been sleeping with a student and several students have also come forward to say you have slept with them. Though you have immensely contributed to the University's growth and development by your good counsel and excellent teaching skills, we however, cannot have someone who endangers the lives and interests of students in this University. As a result we hereby state that you will no longer serve as a lecturer in this university and you will no longer be recognized as a representative or ambassador of this University. We wish you goodluck in your next endeavor," the communications coordinator read out.

Their words were final and there was nothing he could do about it.

"I'm ashamed of you," one woman who had helped him in the pursuit of his academic career told him before she left in a huff.

"You are a disgrace, James," another colleague stated as he bowed his head.

"I'm glad this happened…you deserved this," his wife came up to him and said with a lingering smile, "And now I can choose to leave."

In a matter of minutes, the news was all over campus. A lecturer had been sacked, and that lecturer had been no other person than, Prof. Bediako. He was stripped off of all his respect and entitlement in the University and his wife sought divorce.

Even though Dorcas was happy and glad Prof. Bediako was sacked, she still found it difficult to study. So she sought Sompa's help. Day after day and gradually, Sompa helped her with her studies. It was tough for Dorcas but soon she got the hang of it.

On Thursday evening after so many days of burning the midnight candle and doing till day break, Dorcas found herself at Fawohodie Park. The people she had asked told her that she will find him here. It was a beautiful park with the botanical gardens on the side and a big stadium and race track. It looked absolutely beautiful at night and it held the music of various people praying to God.

In the past, she would have told these people off, but now she was here to see him. She was told that they normally met at the gardens at 6.30pm and as she neared the place she could already hear someone praying loudly.

"Kadinima, Kadinima, Ebaaa Ebaa, Ebabaaaa!" The person who looked very much like Steven paced about, deep in prayer. She went closer and wondered if she should break his prayer chain but tapped him on his shoulder on second thought.

He opened his eyes and saw her and he was pleasantly surprised.

"Dorcas…" he began and she watched as a smile slowly broke out on his face. His happiness was palpable, "Didn't expect to see you here."

"Didn't expect to see myself here either."

"Why are you here?" He asked as he led her to sit on a bench.

"I want to get my life right ok? I don't know where to start from and I thought of you…"

"Glad you came to me, Dorcas, I will help you with that…oh the others are here! Let me introduce you to them."

"Welcome guys, Dorcas meet my fellow members; this is Nana Adwoa, Kate, Mary, Nii and Roland. More people will be joining us soon."

"Nice to meet you."

"Nice to meet you too," they said with a welcoming smile.

"Dorcas will be joining us to pray, so Dorcas we are going to take it one step at a time, ok?" He said as he looked at her.

"Ok."

"Now we can begin…Let us begin to pray in the language of the Spirit." After five long minutes of forever, Steven spoke again and Dorcas sighed in relief.

"God said in Joel chapter 2 that He is going to restore to you the years the locusts have eaten," He declared in a commanding prayerful voice, "Repeat after me and say, in the name of Jesus."

"In the Name of Jesus."

"I cannot hear you, say it again, in the name of Jesus."

"In the name of Jesus."

"By fire by force."

"By fire by force."

"Any locust that has been sent to consume me…"

"Any locust that has been sent to consume me…"

"Any locust that has been sent to destroy me."

"Any locust that has been sent to destroy me."

"Any crawling locust hat has been sent to waste my years."

"Any crawling locust hat has been sent to waste my years."

"Shall be exterminated."

"Shall be exterminated."

"Now clap your hands and pray! Pray for restoration, pray!" He urged.

Dorcas still felt out of place as she mumbled a prayer. She furtively opened her eyes as she watched the people around praying with all seriousness. She noticed how much their number had increased and closed her eyes again. This was definitely not her thing but she would learn. This was good in a strange different way.

———————————————

"Araba, someone is here to see you," called Maame.

"Who is it?" She was at the balcony preparing some stews and soups for the week. She just hoped it wasn't a guy she needed to impress because right now she smelled like *momoni*.

"Come to the room."

"Uhmmm ok."

She hurriedly cleaned the sweat on her forehead and lowered the stove and she went to the room with the napkin still around her neck.

When she saw her, she wanted to scream but all she could do was whisper as if shouting will make her disappear.

"Mama."

"Araba, my dear," her mother said in the warm voice she recognized. She opened her arms for a hug and Araba run into them.

"Oh Mama, you are back."

"Yes dear I am back and I am so sorry for leaving," her mother said, tears spilling as she continued to rub her back, "So sorry I zoned out after Esaaba died. How could I forget that I had another child who was still alive? I'm so sorry, my dear."

"It's okay Mama, I miss her too," she said as she looked into her mother's eyes with a smile.

"We've got each other and Esaaba is forever in our hearts."

"Yes she is. We are all going to meet someday." Her mother promised, "I'm sorry I couldn't handle my grief well and it affected all of you at home."

"It's fine, Mama. I'm just glad you are better now."

"What is that delicious aroma I am smelling? Who is spoiling our noses in this room?"

"Mummy, it's your daughter o," Maame spoke up, teasing.

"Then I came at the right time paa."

"Hahaaaa yes Mama you surely did." She was so happy.

"Serve me some of that momoni goodness before I leave."

"Sure it's ready." For Araba, this was her testimony. Her heart was now full.

CHAPTER SIXTEEN

Perfect flaws

Sompa struggled everyday with people's perceptions about her and the pictures and video that seemed to rear their ugly heads anytime someone passed snide comments. She learnt to be strong with the support of her friends and her family.

As days passed and weeks turned into months, Sompa gradually broke out of her sad state and blossomed into a flower. Together with Naomi, Nolan and Dorcas, she founded a Non Governmental Organisation called Stay Alive to Save a Life which was an organization for people living with depression, mental illness and to help people who were filled with thoughts of suicide. One of the goals was to create awareness about the condition and to help people who were in the position she had been through.

Nolan spent a great amount of time with Sompa and made sure to help her with the responsibilities of the foundation, that way, he also got to spend a lot of time with her.

"Eii you, don't you have a meeting with your supervisor?" Sompa suddenly asked when they were drafting some letters to be sent to Senior High schools next week for their upcoming Mental Health Day.

"I do but that will be later, plus you know I'm done with my project now so I'm just going to hand over the thesis for him to sign and then I'll submit it."

"Wow, you finished early. I know of some final years who are now starting theirs."

"That's because I started early." He said laughingly, "You know you have to start thinking of your final year project."

"Boi, don't come and gimme pressure I just started the course o," Sompa said in mock annoyance.

"I know paa, good reason for you to start soon. I could help you."

"Shark baako p3!" Sompa remarked, looking up at him with a smile, "Thanks, really Nolan for being there for me."

"You are welcome, dear Sompa." Nolan stared unashamedly at her and took her hand in his. "Sompa, I have something to tell you. I've been meaning to tell you ever since I met you and you became my sister's bestfriend. I really like you, I know that you may probably not fully recover from what happened, but I just want to let you know that I'll be here to hug those scars, I'll be here to help you through all of it."

"Wow, I like you too…didn't know you liked me."

"Well, now you know," he said with a smile, relieved and thankful.

"Heheheeee, but why do you like me, I'm damaged goods now. I have not fully forgiven myself just yet. I was taught to how to forgive someone and to ask for forgiveness but never how to give it to myself. My videos and pictures are all over social media. My image is being crucified, I'm no longer the 'virtuous' woman I once was. Sometimes I go on social media to read people's comments under the video and pictures and they are just enough to make me want to empty a box of pills and end it all again but I've learnt to be kind to my mind. People will probably hate you for dating me."

"I don't care what people think. I know you and I know that incident was very unfortunate but that does not make you damaged goods. There is always a reason for things like this. I'm not saying that if you hadn't gone through this perhaps you wouldn't even be starting your own NGO but that's life. Things happen and we've got to find that silver lining in the dark cloud."

"I guess I've found that silver lining now," she said smiling and looking at him.

"And what is it?" He asked, already knowing the answer.

"You."

Nolan's heart warmed and leapt with joy at once as he reached out to hug her.

"C'mon, you have worked too hard. Let's go get some gobε and ice cream."

"That combi sounds so sinful," she said, looking up at him and getting up, "But it's at the Broad way…those guys are bound to say things to me."

"Don't worry, I'll be by your side," Nolan took her hand in his and walked out the door with her.

Glossary

eii	- exclamation used when one is surprised
aden	- why
Anaa	- or
commer	- commercial
gyae gimmie no	- stop the fooling
kaikai	- scary
Lady ena wo nante te se dabodabo	- You are lady and you are walking like a duck
etwii obi	- it is pricking someone's conscience
Oh gyae me	- leave me alone
dumsor	- light off and on
gobe	- plantain and beans
pɛ	- only
anka menfa ma wo	- like I won't give it to you
Hwɛ ne shoes	- Look at her shoes

dadabee	- someone who lives in a comfortable home where everything is provided
zomi	- red oil
yawaad	- disgraced
Sore, sore na wa da kakraa eye	- it is okay, wake up, you have slept enough
Cadaver	- corpse
Tweaa	- term used to snub/disregard a statement
Ashawo	- prostitute
momoni	- smelly, salted fish used in some Ghanaian dishes

Selassie Mensah is a young lady who is passionate about reading and writing. She is a young Ghanaian author who wrote and published her first novel of 200 pages at the age of 14 titled, "The Broom." She also has a storybook for children called, "Reach for the Sun." She has written a lot of short stories for the Bubbles Magazine, which is a magazine by young writers and for children. She also has several stories, poems and articles on her blog, www.selassiespeaksblog.wordpress.com.

In 2010, she won the Citi Fm Write Away Contest and was honoured as the Youngest Achiever in 2012. She shares her passion for reading and writing through the establishment of book clubs in various schools. Selassie is inspired by what goes on around her and expresses and changes perceptions using the power of the pen.